SAMARITAN
ADVENTURER

SAMARITAN
ADVENTURER

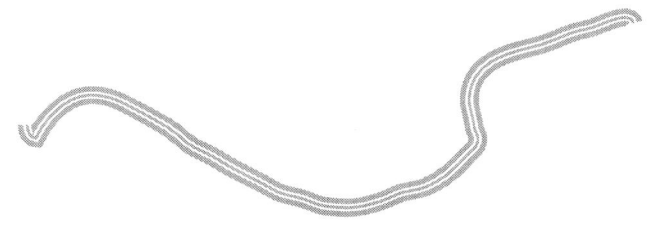

TREVOR JONES

Copyright © 2017 by Trevor Jones

All rights reserved. No part of this book may be reproduced, scanned, or distributed in any printed or electronic form without permission from the publisher.

This is a work of fiction. Names, characters, places, events, and incidents are either the product of the author's imagination or are used fictitiously. The author's use of places or businesses is not intended to change the entirely fictional character of the work. In all other respects, any resemblance to persons living or dead, businesses, companies, events, or locales is entirely coincidental.

ISBN: 978-0-692-82838-0

Printed in the United States of America
First Edition

COVER AND TEXT DESIGN BY MARY JO ZAZUETA
WWW.TOTHEPOINTSOLUTIONS.COM

SAMARITAN
ADVENTURER

Prologue

MY WIFE, KAY, PASSED AWAY ON OCTOBER 15, 2015. After four years of intense back pain and wasting away to ninety pounds, she just gave up. She was seventy-nine.

During this time, I quit my job and cared for Kay 24/7. We tried to receive hospice care in her last remaining months; finally on the third try, we received the care we both needed. Kay lived only forty-five days after hospice took over. By that time, I was a wreck, both physically and mentally.

About the first of October, she just gave up and stopped eating and drinking. For her last fifteen days, she starved herself to death. On the 17th of October, our fifty-sixth wedding anniversary, I buried her in Kalamazoo. By her wishes, the internment was quiet and peaceful, with only a small gathering of relatives and friends in attendance.

I had been the manager at Northport Hardware for thirty-two years; so many people knew Kay and me. They shared their condolences on my loss and wanted me to return to the hardware store so I could again help solve their problems. These friends knew Kay well and missed her, but they also knew she was much happier now after suffering through four years of intense pain.

Even though I knew thousands of families all over the

world face similar losses, closure on Kay's death was a challenge. Being home without her was a major change, and peace was not forthcoming.

Eventually I came to the conclusion that a change of scenery was in order. I would take a road trip through the rough snow country along Lake Superior. Having to focus on the weather and road conditions would keep my mind occupied and off of my remorse. I would break up my travel by stopping in the small villages and hamlets along the route to visit with the local folks and hear of their life experiences. Some would be comical, some sad, and some might be told for the first time.

I would start with the Upper Peninsula of Michigan. I would seek out and talk with people to learn what they had done in their lifetimes. That would be my adventure. Whatever happened each day, would be written in a logbook. And those records were a godsend when I sat down to write *Samaritan Adventurer*.

Although I hope you can visualize yourself beside me, riding in the passenger seat or sitting at a table with four senior gentlemen telling stories of their past—above all, remember, this is a novel. And, like most novels, some things are true; others are not.

PART I

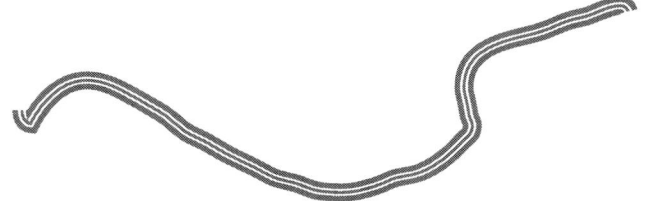

Chapter 1

THE LAST TIME I BOWLED WAS OVER THIRTY-FIVE years ago, in 1979, when I finished the season with a 187 average. It would be fun spending time with the guys. I had kept my two bowling balls and shoes—I found them while I was sorting through stuff in the basement after Kay died.

I brought them upstairs and tried to open the bag, to no avail. The zipper had seized up and would not move. I could hardly grip the zipper tab. I got a pair of pliers and tried again. No luck. This was getting to be a real problem. I went to my workshop in the pole barn. It was a mess, like the house had been. I located my bottle of Marvel Mystery Oil, returned to the house, and lubricated the whole zipper. It would take a while for the oil to do its thing; so a cup of coffee might ease my frustration.

The stuck zipper was a reminder of all the other problems I encountered while sorting through stuff.

After a cup of coffee, I went back to the zipper. With pliers in hand, I twisted, turned, pushed, and pulled—to no avail. Again and again (I didn't keep count), I tried to move the zipper. Finally, it seemed to move a touch. I backed it up and tugged again, until it moved half an inch. I took an old piece of t-shirt and wiped the corrosion and oil from the zipper, re-oiled it, and continued working the zipper up and down until I got it to the top of the bag where it curved to go across the top. It didn't want to make the turn; so back to pushing and pulling again.

I had to hold on to both sides of the bag with one hand while trying to move the zipper with the other. I was gaining on it, when the stitching that held the zipper to the bag broke. After a few (maybe more) unkind words, I finally got the bag unzipped. An hour and a half had been spent on this task. No wonder it takes people, especially seniors, so long to get anything done.

The bag was now open and the shoes were neatly tucked around the ball. I removed the shoes. Oh, my! The toes were turned up and they looked like a pair of elf shoes. Back then (1950s) shoes were made of leather; and after so many years in storage, the leather had dried out and shrunk. Another problem to deal with.

Leather conditioner, shoe trees, and time would solve this problem. I could purchase leather conditioner at a shoe store or maybe, if lucky, at the village supermarket.

Somewhere in the house I had a pair of shoes trees, but where? I hadn't seen them while sorting stuff in the basement, so they must be tucked away upstairs—maybe in my bedroom closet with the extra shoes. Off to my bedroom.

I soon realized that closet floors are a great place to put stuff! Three pairs of shoes with cracks, dirt from the yard, and holes big enough to let water get inside and soak your feet. The kind of shoes that are so comfortable you just can't part with them.

I removed the shoestrings that looked reusable, tied them together, and set them off to one side. In sorting through stuff in the house earlier, I kept finding shoelaces, one pair at a time, in every nook, cranny, and box; to the point I found an old shoebox and labeled it SHOE STRINGS on both ends. That box was now in my barn across the street, so these reclaimed ones would have to be put away later.

On hands and knees, my head again in the closet, I started to search for those shoe trees. Ha! Something wood. It felt like a shoe tree. Nope! Not so lucky—it was a shoe stretcher. (If you ask a kid, or even an adult under forty, to describe a shoe tree or a shoe stretcher, they would think you are nuts and pulling their leg.) I set the shoe stretcher off to the side, by the shoestrings, and continued fishing around in the closet. This time I felt two wooden blocks, which were the two shoe trees.

A simple process of opening a bowling bag had turned into a semi-major operation. Crawling to my bed and gripping it to raise myself off the floor, I decided I needed a break. Another cup of coffee and sitting down would do.

After my break, I slipped—well, more like shoved—the shoe trees into the shoes and rubbed on several coats of leather conditioner, which I had surprisingly found in a cabinet. I'd check the shoes in a few days to see if they had flattened out.

In late October, I received a phone call from one of the co-directors of the Northport Community Band. They being Ken Bloomquist and Don Wilcox. Ken was retired from Michigan State University as their band director and Don was retired from the University of West Virginia, as their band director. Both were known nationally in the collegiate community. Their great sense of humor in leading this gathering of guys and gals, who like me hadn't played an instrument in fifty years, went a very long way in helping us play entertaining music. We played lots of marches and some tough music compositions. The tough songs, being sight read for the first time, would be terrible and many accomplished members would groan and moan: "I can't play this piece up to speed." With a firm look, Ken or Don would say, "Well, it's a start. Let's try the first six bars again."

Being invited to rejoin the band—I had left the group five years earlier—was such a wonderful compliment I couldn't turn it down. When I joined the band at their first practice session for the Christmas Concert, Don introduced me and I received a rousing welcome from everyone, even those who had joined after I had left five years before. Even though I played like a novice, it was great to get back into the band.

After the Christmas Concert, the band is inactive until the third week of April; so that activity would end. I traveled to Kalamazoo and spent Christmas Eve with my niece and her family, and Christmas night with eight of Kay's cousins and their families. Happy times like in the past, but not as good as if Kay had been there.

I was still trying to cope with Kay's death after fifty-six years of marriage. It takes time when your spouse is suddenly not a part of your daily life. I had always been active, with something going on; projects, some of them small, some large; building, cleaning, and staining the deck; re-roofing the house; snow removal of the driveways, house and barn roofs; and all the other things that go into maintaining a home. But I was kind of at loose ends. Just sitting, contemplating what to do. Not watching TV (98 percent was junk programs), trying to figure out what was going on with me. The future wasn't looking very bright.

I realized I needed to do something, but what? I wasn't lacking for anything in the house, didn't need any new autos. I had Susie, my 1998 Suburban, in great running order even with 233,000 miles; Kay's 1975 Chevrolet pickup, with only 54,000 miles and not fully broken in; and my 2005 Dodge

Caravan, with 150,000 miles. In the 1930s and 40s an engine usually needed overhauling at 65,000 miles. Today, if autos are serviced regularly with new oil filter, repairs to the little things that wear out, and repairing the body rust before it gets of out hand, a vehicle can travel 400,000 miles without major repairs.

I have to do something.

Finally, I realized an adventure of some sort might be in order. My community of Northport was pretty low-key. Everybody was friendly and always waves or says hello—whether they know you or not. Everybody walks their dogs and when people stop to pet them, if they have a dog treat in their pocket, they will give the dog a treat or two.

I had spent almost all of my adult life in retail sales and, when time permitted, enjoyed chatting with my customers on any subject, except politics and religion. You can learn so much by chatting with people: hobbies, what they are doing, sports they like, and the list goes on and on. Maybe an extended road trip across part of the country would be fun. Instead of traveling the interstate highways, I would stay off the beaten track. In the small towns that dot the country, I could drop in on the guys' morning coffee sessions at the local bakery or restaurant, where any number of subjects would be hashed over and nothing resolved. A good icebreaker would be to ask what high school sports were coming up that I could attend. In the northern states, hockey and basketball are a really big deal in high school, and the admission cost is nominal.

The more I thought about it, the more a road trip appealed to me. It could turn out to be an adventure.

Chapter 2

THE DECISION WAS MADE AND THE PLANNING AND preparation began. First was making a list of where I wished to travel and specific cities I would drive through or be near—a basic itinerary—so I could tell my AAA travel agent where I wanted to go. My list included: Sault Ste. Marie and Copper Harbor in Michigan's Upper Peninsula; then Duluth, Minnesota; Mt. Rushmore in South Dakota; Laramie, Wyoming; Denver and Colorado Springs in Colorado; Albuquerque and Roswell, New Mexico; David City, Nebraska; and Iowa City, Iowa. Eleven states in all and about four thousand miles.

It was going to take some time to gather the state maps, a TripTik, and tour guides for lodging and restaurant information. I would put the travel material from AAA in a small box to keep it in one spot.

I called my AAA travel agent, Lori, and told her what I had in mind and that it would be an extended trip. I asked her to hold everything at her office and to call me when it was ready. I would drive to her office in Traverse City to pick it up. She said it would be about ten 10 days, which was fine with me.

Three days later, she called. What fast service that was.

The next day, I picked up the information. It was neatly sorted in three plastic bags. The box would work terrifically.

On my drive back home, I felt a premonition of what I was going to do and my heart started beating fast. My heart-rate is normally about as fast as a turtle walks, and my pulse jumped to at least sixty beats a minute. (A nurse once told me I should live to be 100 years old because my heart would never wear out. Well, I'm eighty-five; she might be right.)

My intent was to stop at the villages, towns, and hamlets that paralleled the basic interstate route and visit with the people who lived there; to learn about their heritage, why the town came to be, etc., and record the stories they told. From visiting such communities in the past, I knew the best people to chat with are waitresses, hardware store clerks, morning coffee drinkers, and patrons at bars or pubs in the afternoon and during evening happy hour. Leading questions will usually get people started talking; otherwise I'd ask if they wanted to hear a story of mine. Folks who live in small communities, especially senior citizens, will tell a story, usually funny or comical, and once they started, they'd really get into it. A big bonus was that when two or three (or more) seniors were together, they would each try to outdo the previous storyteller.

~ ~ ~

A good hardware store clerk—I was one for thirty-two years—develops a knack for asking questions. "May I help you?" wasn't always the best way to open a conversation. One axiom in a hardware store is that every customer has a problem and it's the clerk's job to provide a solution: either how-to instructions or, if you don't have everything needed for the task, then readily tell the customer where they can obtain it. I guess I was pretty good at this because many of my customers would walk into the store and say, "Boy, am I'm glad you're here! Just the man I want to see."

That type of greeting always made me feel good. Some customers were lost when trying to explain their problem and when I offered to stop by their house after work to size things up, they appreciated it—and it made for lasting friendships. Note: if every time you, as a customer, walk into a business and greet the clerk or other staff person with "I'm glad you're here!"—he will do his best to help you with your needs.

~ ~ ~

My planning list included categories such as: clothing for cold and warm temperatures; food for snacks, appropriate cookware; and emergency items, including a first aid kit. Camera, cell phone, and a GPS device should also be packed. Individual items were listed under each category until I felt everything required would be remembered. As I gathered each item, I placed it in the backroom at the entrance to the house from the driveway. I would accumulate quite a pile of stuff by the time I was done. Not a pretty sight for someone coming to visit—but what the heck? People would come to see me not my stuff.

When everything was checked off on the list, I backed Susie up to the entrance and started packing her. I had everything in except extra water and food that might freeze. Somehow I was even able to leave enough room in the back to roll out my sleeping bag if I decided to sleep in Susie overnight somewhere. I would start out the next morning, well rested and raring to go.

Sleeping was impossible that night. My mind was racing over and over on what was packed, what was being forgotten, and the whole trip in general.

Chapter 3

I WAS LEAVING SAULT STE. MARIE, HEADING WEST along the route that had been laid out by Lori. Periodically, I stopped at villages and hamlets along the way. Although many of the stops were interesting and I had a good time, I hadn't had a good conversation with anybody yet. I seemed to be having a hard time getting my act together and getting the guys in the shops to talk—but I'd keep on plugging along.

I stopped at the Point Iroquois Lighthouse and Museum. It was closed. I would probably find many points of interest closed, since it was winter and the weather in the U.P. can be harsh, especially along the Lake Superior shoreline.

The stretch from Sault Ste. Marie to Marquette is the perfect setting for winter activities. Caravans of snowmobilers, skiers, and dogsled teams flock to the area. It is beautiful. This time of year—December, January, February, and March—is the busiest season for the businesses in this area. Without the winter revelers, the people in the U.P. would really have it rough financially.

I pulled into a small town to see if I could find lodging for the night. I stopped at a small motel and asked the clerk if there was a room available. He just laughed and said,

"Mister, this is the busiest week of the year. Every room is filled—business or private." I hadn't thought of this situation when planning my excursion. I immediately decided that the first thing to do was get Susie filled up with fuel; then I'd drive a ways, stop at the side of the road and rest a bit, and then drive on a little farther. Even though it was cold outside, by doing this, it would keep Susie fairly warm while I rested. Because of her size, Susie has two heaters: a front one with a defroster and a rear heater.

I asked the motel clerk where the town's gas station was located. He said, "Where all the snowmobiles and trucks are parked. The bars are mostly farther out of town."

There must be 100 snowmobiles and a lot of pickup trucks, all lined up to use the three gas pumps. I got out of Susie and walked up to the truck in front me and asked the driver if this was the line for the gas pumps. He replied, "Sure is! And it's going to take a while to get to them. The snowmobilers have to first add oil to the tank and then fill the tank with gas."

I looked at my watch. It was 8 p.m. I hoped the gas station stayed open late. I turned Susie off and sat back to wait it out. Slowly the line moved forward, only to stop again. This repeated for an hour. I was getting closer to the gas pumps. Finally, I pulled forward to the second pump and thank goodness there were two nozzles on each pump. I got out, flipped open the gas door, removed the gas cap, and inserted the nozzle and started pumping gas.

Usually I pay for gas with cash, but with the waiting line still beyond sight, the honorable thing to do was use a credit card and get out of the way. When Susie was gassed up, I pulled off to an open spot, parked, and went inside the store and paid my bill. There wasn't much going on in the store so I started looking over the snacks and the soda cooler.

An older lady, the owner of the store, came over and asked if she could help. I told her of my dilemma and that it was going to be a long night for me. She piped right back and said, "I won't have it! I have an extra bedroom that is all set. You are going to stay at my house tonight. I'm going home at ten o'clock; you can follow me there."

I could hardly believe my ears. Opening up her house to a total stranger!

~ ~ ~

A similar situation happened back in the 1960s when two of my buddies and I were deer hunting near Luther, Michigan. It had been raining off and on all day, our hunting clothes were soaked, and we planned to sleep in the Suburban we rode in. With wet clothing, it was going to be a miserable night for us.

One of the fellow's had a wife who was expecting to deliver in about a week; so he wanted to call and check on her. There was one pay phone in Luther and it had a line of guys waiting to use it. Everything was okay with his wife and, after chatting for a few minutes, he hung up and we went inside the warm store in hopes that our hunting suits would dry out some. We were in no hurry, and just poked around the store, with our hunting jackets fully unzipped so the insides would dry some, taking our sweet, merry old time.

An older woman (older than the three of us) seemed to sense that something was amiss. She asked us if there was a problem. We told her we had driven up from Allegan and planned on sleeping in the Suburban. But the rain all day soaked our clothing and we were using the heat in the store to dry out our clothing a bit. We told her that this was our fourth year hunting in Luther and that the trailer we had used before was sold, so sleeping in the car was the plan. She said, "No way are you guys going to sleep in wet clothing—even if is only 34 degrees. I have two empty bedrooms with double beds. You're going to sleep at my house tonight."

We were astonished at such a wonderful offer and told her we would gladly pay whatever amount she wanted. She said, "I don't want any pay! I take pleasure in helping people who are in a bad fix. I'm closing shop at ten. I have to open up tomorrow morning. Wait for me by the door at ten and you can follow me home."

Upon entering her home, we commenced taking off our boots. She said, "Leave them on!"

We explained we couldn't get out of our wet hunting suits without taking our boots off, and besides, they were wet also. "We'll set them off to the side with the suits."

She replied, "Remove your compasses and empty the pockets. I'll run them through the clothes dryer. What time do you guys want to get up?"

"When it's of no inconvenience to you," was our reply.

"I'll give you a holler at six," she said, and showed us to our rooms on the second floor.

At six the next morning, we heard the call to rise and shine. We made the beds, left substantial tips underneath our pillows, and then went down to the kitchen. Bacon, eggs, coffee, and toast were being prepared by her for the three of us, her husband, and herself. Our hunting suits were neatly folded and on another table off to the side. We put on our dry hunting suits and boots and thanked her several times. All three of us gave her a big hug. She was beaming with delight that she had invited us into her home. None of us had ever heard of this happening to anyone before—and now, it was happening to me again!

~ ~ ~

The lady showed me to the room I was to sleep in. I told her to wake me up when she did and I would be on my way. I thanked her again for her wonderful hospitality.

The next morning, after she called me, I dressed, made up the bed, put a tip for her underneath the pillow, and went downstairs to the smell of coffee, bacon, eggs, and toast. What a marvelous Good Samaritan had come into my life again.

After eating, I put on my boots, offered to pay her—which she turned down—and warmly thanked her before heading out the door. I started up Susie, backed out of the driveway, waved goodbye and headed to town to continue my adventure.

Chapter 4

NEXT ON MY LIST: GRAND MARAIS, PICTURED ROCKS National Lakeshore, Marquette, and Copper Harbor.

The weather was not the best, but not bad enough to be a serious hindrance either. In Pictured Rocks, the roads to the shoreline had not been plowed; so I continued westward toward Marquette. I wasn't going to get caught again without a full tank of gas. Marquette would be a good place to fill up Susie and have some pancakes and sausage for my lunch before heading north to Copper Harbor.

Copper Harbor is an isolated town at the tip of the Keweenaw Peninsula, much the same as Northport is on the Leelanau Peninsula, except Keweenaw juts into Lake Superior some sixty miles or so. It has rugged, forested terrain and is a pretty drive in the summer—it should be equally beautiful now, with the evergreen trees tipped white with snow. In several spots, I pulled off to the side of the highway to take some photos and take in the beauty of the snow-capped trees. When I arrived at Copper Harbor, I drove out to the State Park Ranger Station, not expecting it to be open in the dead of winter. Surprisingly, a ranger was on duty. He must have been watching out a window because he came out of the building and yelled, "Hello, stranger!"

"Hello, old buddy!" I answered.

He asked if there was something he could do for me. Because he had not put on a jacket, I suggested we go inside his office where it was warmer. After rubbing his hands up and down on his upper arm he agreed. "It has warmed up now, though. It was negative ten last night."

Once we were inside the station, I told him who I was, where I lived, and that I was on an adventure to try to get my life back to normal. He said, "This is as good a place as any to freeze all of the bad things in us." He explained he was transferred up here three years ago. "And although it does get a little lonely in the winter, it sure beats struggling with the high temperatures and humidity downstate in the summer."

I asked if he was from downstate. "Yah, Jackson," he said. "After high school, I spent four years in the Coast Guard, got discharged, and attended U of M and received a degree in forest management. I could have gone to Michigan State, but because U of M was closer, I could live at home.

"I signed on with the Department of Natural Resources after graduation, and they've stationed me all over the state, almost always in parks along the shorelines of Michigan and Huron. Probably because of my service in the Coast Guard. I keep busy varnishing the camp's picnic tables, etc. and plowing snow."

"It must get busier in the summer though," I said.

"Oh, yah. About 50,000 visitors, campers, and people who want to catch the ferry to Isle Royale National Park," he said.

"I was at Isle Royale in August 1945. Had a great time with about twenty-five other Boy Scouts," I shared. "The week after we left Isle Royale, the National Park Service took control of the island and transferred it from State of Michigan control to the National Park Service.

"How do you know it was 1945?" he asked.

"Because seven of us hiked cross country from Isle Royale Harbor south to Lake Michigan. They had had a forest fire there in the early 1930s so there were fallen trees all that were hidden by broad leaf ferns. Three of us got separated from the other four who had the compass and flashlights. Each of us led the way at times, until our shins hurt from walking into the fallen trees.

"We finally reached the harbor, saw some of our fellows hiking on a trail across the bay, and yelled out to them so that they could tell the camp counselors where we were. The water was too cold to walk in barefoot and the brush was too thick to get through along the shoreline. It was almost dark and we could see our campsite fires at the end of the harbor. We yelled to our campsite and they told us to stay put and they would send out a rescue party. We all sat down and leaned against a tree. We were all exhausted and I fell sound asleep.

"The rescue party found us about midnight. One of the counselors said he had been shaking me for ten minutes before I woke up. All of us finally got to the campsite about 2:30 a.m. Everybody learned from that experience that trail hiking was okay, but no more cross country hiking would be allowed.

"The week after I returned home, my high school football team started practice and my shins were all scabbed over and the nerves in my shins were still numb. That fall was the start of my freshman year, so that is how I know what year it was."

The ranger said the park still doesn't allow cross country hiking.

I asked him if he had heard anything about the unexplained copper mines on Isle Royale. He said the last word was Maya Indians from Central America had possibly dug them for the copper.

I explained that if I heard enough stories and had enough interesting conversations like he and I just had, I might write a book about my experiences. "I plan to call it The Adventure. And you would be in it." He said that if the book was ever published, he wanted a signed copy.

Because the snow was too deep snow for me to get to the lakeshore, I decided to spend the night in Ironwood. I gave him a business card from when I had a sideline craft business.

"Now, I have to do bookwork and enter you as being a visitor," he said. "When the home office sees I had a visitor in January, they will want to know what kind of nut visits Copper Harbor in January."

"If they ask, just say some old geezer from Northport got mixed up in his directions and headed north instead of south like everybody else in the Lower Peninsula," I replied.

We shook hands, I climbed into Susie, and headed south toward Ironwood. I arrived in Ironwood just before dark. I rented a room at a motel, gassed up Susie, ate dinner, and returned to the motel. After bringing my logbook up to date on the day's travel, I stretched my legs and turned in for the night.

Chapter 5

THE NEXT MORNING, MY KNEE JOINTS AND BACK were a bit sorer than usual; probably from sitting behind the steering wheel for so many miles without stopping, getting out, and walking around to loosen up.

I put on my felt-pack snow boots, grabbed my camera and light meter, and headed out the door. It was still dark, but with the snow there was enough light for me to see. I walked to the end of the motel. In addition to the snow-covered terrain, I saw a small shed a couple hundred yards out in a field. It was kind of stupid, but I started wading through the snow toward the building. I didn't walk right up to the building, but stayed about twenty feet or so from it and walked around to the other side. Then I turned around and looked behind me. I saw different shaped objects, like boxes and cylinders, all snow-covered. It finally dawned on me: I was standing in a trash dump and the objects were old washing machines and refrigerators. What a place to take a walk!

It had gotten lighter outside; the sun was beginning to rise. I noticed rays of sunlight shining through the shed's vertical-slat siding. I quickly got out my camera and set the setting for wide open and lined myself up with the sun, with the shed blocking out the sun's rays to the camera lens. The weeds in the dump were taller than the snow, so they stuck out of the snow and would be in the picture as well. There was brightness around the shed and subdued light off to each side. At the time, I thought it was going to be a strange picture, but when I had the color print developed, I discovered probably the prettiest photo I had ever taken. The mood of contrasting light bordered by shadows was beautiful. I had it enlarged to an 8 x 10.

I retraced my footsteps in the snow back to my motel room; took off my felt packs, which had a good amount of snow in them; and put on dry socks and my travel shoes. Usually it takes two cups of coffee for me to become alert, but not this morning. I was shaved, checked out of the motel, and on the road toward Duluth in record time.

~ ~ ~

Sometimes, out of the blue, a strange feeling passes over me. For example, twice while talking with total strangers, I blurted out their last names. They stared at me for a few seconds and then asked how I knew their last names. I told them I had absolutely no idea. Other times, something would occur that would be a total surprise—like I had an inward sense of telepathy—a thought or premonition that something was going to happen. In retrospect, I think this phenomena occurred when I didn't drink my usual two cups of coffee to start the day. There was nothing I could do about it but carry on as if it hadn't happened. A wait-and-see attitude.

~ ~ ~

After driving down the highway a short distance, suddenly the feeling came over me. It told me to stop, back up, and turn left onto the road I had just passed. I did what my mind told me to do; and just as suddenly, the feeling disappeared.

This is weird, I thought. Something is going to happen ahead of me and I don't know what. This was a sudden turn of events that I had to investigate.

Chapter 6

I WAS TRAVELING WEST ON HIGHWAY 169 AND HAD already driven through the town of Gurney and Copper Falls State Park, when lo and behold, I saw a sign that read: "Welcome to Mellen"—and I got that feeling again.

When I eased into the town, another sign suddenly jumped out at me: Maggie's Diner. The feeling vanished just as quickly. I decided to cruise through Mellen to see what it was like. There was the usual assortment of shops, a couple of motels, bed and breakfasts, a four-pump gas station, and several bars and eateries. The town was much like Suttons Bay in Leelanau County, Michigan.

I returned to Maggie's Diner. I parked in an alley at the side of the diner, put my pocket recorder in my jacket pocket, and entered the restaurant. There were a few guys sitting on stools at the counter; a few other tables with men eating breakfast; and a large, round table with four older men chatting and drinking coffee from mugs. An older woman, probably in her late fifties, stepped toward me and greeted me with, "Good morning, love. Sit wherever you'd like."

She had a slight accent, but what really got my attention was her use of the word *love*. *Love* was seldom used in our country. She turned around to attend to one of the tables when I sort of burped out, "You're not native-born, are you?"

She turned back toward me and asked how I knew. I avoided answering her question and instead said, "You're from New Zealand or Australia, aren't you?"

I had her attention. She replied, "Australia."

I cut her off and said, "Sidney or Melbourne?" I really had her attention now. She came over to me and I quickly answered her question. "Once in a while, things come to me that I can't explain. Is your maiden name Hoy, or a relative of that name? Did you live in one of the outlying towns of Sidney?"

With a stern look, she said, "Either you're a mighty good guesser or you've be checking up on me."

"Intuition, I guess, because I haven't been checking up on you. And another guess is your married name is Clark."

She replied, "Mister, if you weren't wearing that Green Bay cap, I'd throw you out of here."

I knew I was really getting to her and that I had better cool her down fast. I hurriedly said, "My wife, Kay, had an Aunt Adele Hoy Shook, who passed away three years ago. She came to the United States to marry a Robert N. Shook, whom she had met during World War II. She was Catholic and the two of them had five girls and five boys. She lived to be eighty-nine years old.

"The Shooks and Kay and I became very close. Adele always greeted me with the word *love* in the phrase. I haven't been addressed by anyone with *love* since she died. You addressing me with *love* instantly brought back memories of her and I just couldn't help myself from asking you those questions. I am very sorry if I upset you."

Her expression softened and she explained that her

mother had also died about three years ago and that her maiden name, indeed, was Hoy. "Small world, isn't it? I guess we were supposed to meet. Where would you like to sit, cousin?"

"I see there are four geezers sitting at that round table and there is an empty chair. If they don't mind, I'd like to sit with them and listen to their gossip."

"Come with me," she said. When we were by the table, she spoke sternly to the men. "This is a cousin of mine, and if you don't treat him kindly, I'll quit fixing that special coffee you drink."

"Please, mister. Won't you join us?"

I told Maggie, "A glass of water and High Test coffee to start, please."

With a smile, she answered, "You'll need High Test if you sit with them very long."

I introduced myself and explained that I lived in Northport, Michigan, and that I was on a trip; stopping off here on my way westward. One of them gave me their names as Henry, Al, Adam, and Ken. They had lived in Mellen all their life.

I took my morning dose of ibuprofen and PreserVision with the water and we all had a good drink of coffee.

I noticed their coffee mugs were a reddish color, although each was a different shape and not as pretty as the one Maggie had given me. I asked why their mugs were different than mine.

Henry popped out with, "Under all the rock and marble in the area, there is a reddish clay. When we were kids, our parents would dig up the clay and make cups, plates, platters, and all sizes of bowls with it. Almost everyone in town was kind of poor and they couldn't afford store-bought dishes. These mugs are from our parents' tableware. Maggie knows what mug belongs to who by its shape. Maggie washes them each day and takes really good care of them so they won't get broken."

"You guys like Maggie a lot, don't you?" I said.

"Yah. And she makes a pot of special coffee every day from a pot that she puts on the stove. Nothing like those things called coffee urns behind her counter. We're the only ones that get coffee from our pot."

"Getting back to your mugs ... You just don't take clay, form it, and then put them to use, do you? You have to fire them in a kiln so they become rigid, right?"

"When our ma's started complaining that they were getting low on dishes, our pa's would all go out and dig some clay and add some stuff to it and would make new dishes. It was Ken's pa that made a kiln out of stone and marble that he had scavenged some years before, and the four of them would place their pottery on racks in the upper part of the kiln, then stoke up the fire pot with dry hardwood, light it, and start sipping beer. None of our families could afford coal, and if the burner part of the kiln was kept stoked, it would do, even if it took longer.

"Like the stockpile of dry hardwood, they had stockpiled a stash of beer. They'd start the kiln Saturday morning and would let it go out about noon on Sunday. They would stay up all night, feeding wood into that kiln and sipping beer all the time. By Sunday noon, they were all pretty tipsy, really drunk, and would stretch out on the ground to let the kiln and newly baked pottery cool off. They would sleep off the beer Sunday afternoon, and about 7 p.m. they'd start coming to. When they started coming to Sunday evening, their heads would be aching something awful and then they would bend over, taking turns removing the pottery one piece at a time.

"Every time the one removing the pottery would bend over to reach into the kiln, he would moan and groan something fearful; then another would take over, removing pottery with the same moaning and groaning. And our ma's would exclaim that if those damn fools wouldn't drink so much beer, they could have emptied the kiln in half an hour at most instead of the two hours it took." Al was now laughing so hard he could hardly speak.

The rest of us were patiently waiting to hear what he was laughing about, when finally, half choking, he continued. "Once I sneaked a steel garbage can outside behind our pa's and hit it hard four times with a mallet. All four pa's jumped to their feet and started screaming bloody murder while grasping their aching heads. I dropped the mallet on the spot and all four of us kids ran straight for the safety and protection of my ma and her kitchen. She asked us what was the matter and we told her what I had done. I've never seen my ma break into such laughter and try to say something to us and start laughing as hard as before. She pointed toward the cookie jar and told us to help ourselves, which we did.

"A little bit later, after she had calmed down enough to talk, she told us not to worry about getting spanked and that she would go after him with her iron frying pan if he tried to spank us.

"She sure saved my hide that day!"

While we were laughing at Al's story, Maggie came over with a huge, blue-porcelain, camp-style coffeepot and refilled our mugs. Thank goodness I still had some of her regular brew in my cup when she refilled it. That coffee, even though it was somewhat diluted, was strong enough to burn all the plaque off my teeth. Their coffee would take some getting used to.

Maggie asked if I was ready for breakfast.

"Yes, please. Hotcakes, eggs, and toast with grape jelly or jam," I said.

Al concluded his story by saying that the mallet disappeared that night and he never could find it until after his pa had died. "I was cleaning out and straightening up the barn and I found it hidden from me." After fifty plus years, he still hadn't forgotten that Sunday evening.

One of them explained that they were kind of like the four bad kids in the neighborhood. They kept the town on edge with the stuff they used to do—nothing really bad, mind you, just stuff.

Adam, who had been fairly quiet, disagreed. "Well—one summer we kind of stepped over the line—and really, it was my fault." Adam started his story. "You guys remember that summer when it was hot and sticky and the fish weren't biting; no matter when we fished, morning, noon, afternoon, or in the evening? We had tried worms, night crawlers, wigglers, crickets, and grasshoppers, and nothing worked. Between all of us, we might catch two fish, and it wasn't worth the time to clean them, and besides getting our hands and clothes all fishy smelling."

Somebody replied that they always had a few days each summer when the fish quit biting—the dog days of summer.

"No, I mean, when we tried everything ... and then I had an inspiration and came up with a plan to get fish. You remember, we all went to my house and we went out to Dad's barn and I got a stick of Dad's dynamite and a fuse?"

That turned them all on. I could tell they all remembered that day. Adam looked at me and said, "Let me explain. I got a stick of dynamite and a long length of fuse and one of you guys grabbed a board and pail and went to our fishing hole at the lake. I tied some twine around the board and, hanging onto the other end, we pushed that board into the lake.

There was a little wind at our back and the board drifted out into the lake. We kind of timed that board's journey and pulled the board back to us. I kind of measured a length of fuse, looked it over, and added a few more inches to what I had and cut the fuse, inserted the fuse into the dynamite, laid the dynamite on the board, and coiled the fuse around the stick of dynamite. One of us lit the fuse and pushed the board out into the lake. The board kept drifting out, with little puffs of smoke over the stick. It seemed like a long time for the fuse to burn and we were all staring at that board when suddenly the loudest explosion I had ever heard rang in our ears.

"We heard a noise behind us, and there came a running about ten town folk yelling, 'Is anybody hurt?' We all knew we were in big trouble because the noise of the explosion had traveled all the way into town and people had heard it. I guess we were kind of dumbfounded and not thinking very fast because we didn't think to run off.

"A couple of womenfolk started looking us over careful and checking us for injuries. We tried to tell them that we were all okay, and they let up on that account. But all hell broke out from the men. They demanded to know what we had done. We sheepishly said we were fishing. 'With dynamite?!' one yelled. I think his hands we're shaking.

"I won't say here what else they said because it was all bad language. Then they said they would tell our folks. Suddenly we all came to life and started to explain we were just trying to learn something. We pleaded with them, saying that if they told our dads our butts would be redder than their red flannels for a week or more and really no good would come of having us kids beat to a pulp. Our pleading was working some. So we said we would take the rowboat on the shore and go out and gather up the dead fish, clean them, and they could have fresh fish for dinner, and that we didn't deserve any because of what we had done.

"They softened up and returned to town. We all got in the rowboat and rowed out to where the dynamite had exploded. Boy, did we have fish! We almost filled that five-gallon pail full of pan fish, perch, and some good bass. What a haul.

"We rowed back to shore, pulled the boat up on the beach, and headed for Adam's house. We had never gotten so many fish before, and that pail was heavy for us little kids. It took two of us to carry that pail to Adam's house."

"What about the board?" I asked.

Their answer was that there wasn't a piece bigger than a little finger and the pieces were spread all over the lake.

"Well, we cleaned that pail of fish in no time with all of us working away at it," Adam continued. "We wanted to deliver the cleaned fish to the town folk and be home before our dads got home from work, when we would all act like it had been a dull day. We delivered the fish to the ten people who had come to the lake and they were happy that we had lived up to our part of the bargain that had been made.

"And, they lived up to their part too because our folks never knew what we had done. Of course, the town was on high alert the rest of the summer. It felt like a pair of eyes was always trained on us."

Maggie came over with more refills. I told her only a half cup please and gave her a wink. She winked back. She knew I was being polite in not turning down a cup of their coffee.

Another story soon began. "We kind of got in trouble with the school teacher ..." They all laughed and agreed it was some time that day, but—

"We were just kids, and we kept getting kicked out of school. We tried to convince our moms that the teacher didn't have much of a sense of humor, but our moms never bought into that. One day, we put our heads together and made a plan for the next day at school.

"Ken had snitched some of his mom's matches; you know, the wooden ones with white tips that when you wanted to light one, you stretched out your leg and wiped the match across the pant leg and the white tip would burst into flame. We were taught not to play with them."

I remarked that they were sulfur matches—the greatest thing in the world, especially for kids.

"Since it was the middle of winter, our plan was to build a small fire inside the Johnny. The outdoor john was a cold honker when you had to go. There were separate johns for the girls and boys; each had four holes—just the right number for the four of us.

"You know, when you had to do your thing, a cold john is not a pleasant place to be. So in our plan, Ken would get the matches and an old steel pail, and Alan and Adam would bring some dry tinder and short pieces of wood. We took the pail, wood, and tinder and hid it behind the john before school started. At the morning break, we all had to go so we grabbed the pail and wood and went into the john. Ken took a match and whipped it across his leg and lit the tinder.

"Now, most people think that the crescent cutouts in the outhouse door were to let the odor out, our thinking was they were to let the smoke out. It wasn't a big fire, but it was making more smoke than we had anticipated. We all had our pants down, getting ready to go, when Ken said, 'Man, I got some good gas,' and we all jumped in and said we did too.

"Anyway, we had a game we liked to play to see who could make the most flame. What that was is one guy held a lighted match at the butt of another one of us who would bend over and let out a big fart; you know, you get the prettiest blue flame—sometimes with a yellow fringe.

"The little fire in the bucket had warmed up the john pretty good so we ended up having a contest to see who could make the biggest blue flame. I don't know if we ever did decide who won because we were interrupted. Somebody must have seen the smoke coming out of the crescent shapes and yelled fire. The schoolteacher came a charging out of the schoolhouse, looked at the john and the smoke pouring out of those crescents, and she yelled, 'Help! Go get the Fire Department!'

"We heard her yelling and one of us opened the door and stuck his head out and yelled at her there was no fire. We were okay. All was under control. We didn't need the fire department. The teacher charged over to the john and yelled, 'What in the world are you doing?'

"There we were, standing in the doorway with our pants down to our ankles, and we thought for sure the whole devil was going to break out on us. The teacher started to stammer and finally blurted out, 'You urchins! Get your pants up, sit at your desk, and I don't want to hear a peep out of any of you!' We knew she was mad; so we did as she ordered and quietly returned to the schoolhouse.

"At the end of the school day, she dismissed the class, but called out our names in an extra-firm voice and said, with the words spaced apart, '**You four stay here**. I'm going to have a talk with you.' We could tell she was still mad.

"When the other kids had left, she walked over to us and looked each of us straight in the eye. Her eyes seemed to be flaming as she said, 'I've had it with you kids. It's one thing after another. But I'm not going to kick you out of school this time—but from here on, none of you go with any of the others. It's one at a time or you don't go at all. Now, have you got that straight?' 'You mean, we can't go to the Johnny?' She replied, 'You can go, but only one at a time. If I catch two of you together, you will be kicked out of school for a week—and you know what your fathers are going to do.' She never did learn about the flame trick."

One of the guys added, "You know, she really gave us a big break that day by not kicking us out of school, because I suddenly felt respect for her, and from then on, I really tried to learn from her and do my homework. And, if I didn't understand whatever she was teaching, I'd stay after school and she would go over my questions and help me until I had an understanding of the material. She was our teacher for three more years, and she always gave me special instruction whenever I needed it. My grades improved and we became good friends."

Chapter 7

AFTER THAT STORY, WE WERE QUIETLY SIPPING OUR coffee, when Maggie came over to the table carrying the big blue coffeepot. "I got to take this thing off the burner. If I leave it on any longer, the coffee will eat the bottom right out of it; so I'm going to refill your mugs and that will be it for the day," she said.

One of the men said, "Be sure our friend gets some too."

Maggie filled up mine first and poured what was left in the four guys' mugs. Everybody had warmed-up coffee. Maggie said she had to go back in the kitchen and get to doing up the dishes. "When you are ready to check out, just give a holler." We all nodded our heads in agreement.

After a couple minutes, all of a sudden, one of the guys blurted out, "Do you remember the opening day of bass season? The night we went fishing?"

The other three guys' chins popped up in the air and they all had funny looks on their faces. One of them said, "Yes, that was a night to remember, wasn't it? There was one of us in the bow, one in the stern, and two in the middle seat of the boat. We were going out in the lake to get ourselves some nice, fresh bass, knowing it was going to be legal this time, with no dynamite."

Another piped in, "And we were in for a surprise, weren't we? Three of us had cane poles with a bobber hooked on above the hook—and, who was it had one of those new fishing rods with a reel?"

Henry jumped in and declared, "That was me! My dad had given it to me for Christmas. He gave me a good one, too. I still have it hanging over my fireplace mantel." He lowered his voice and said, "That was the best Christmas present he ever gave to me."

Another guy added, "We had to keep jigging our cane poles up and down. You, lucky stiff, would sling out that artificial bait way out from the boat and reel it in; sometimes jerking the rod up and making that bait splash in the water. We all envied you because you always caught as many fish as the three of us, until we finally got our own rods and reels."

"But, anyway, you kept casting that plug when you got a strike on your bait," Henry said. "I remember that thing really hit the bait hard and started peeling the line off the reel and I had to cup my hand over the reel handles to stop it from spinning so fast. Gradually I was able to reel it in a little bit and then it would take off again taking more of my line. I remember thinking I really had me a jumbo bass. Brand-new fish line that wouldn't break. I fought that thing for thirty minutes (the others nodded in agreement) and gradually that monster was getting closer to our boat and one of you guys grabbed the big net we had and you other two flashed the water with your flashlights.

"'There it is!' yelled one of you, and I worked that thing closer to the surface and yelled, 'Net him!' and you did and flipped the net and the thing into the rear of the boat."

"'You landed him!' we yelled to Henry—and then all hell broke loose in that net. Henry had hooked a muskrat by the tail—and was that muskrat ever mad! It chewed a hole through our net and attacked you two guys in the middle seat, snapping at your feet, and you both fell backward into the front of the boat to escape that muskrat!"

"Somehow the bait had come unhooked from its tail and it escaped out of the boat," continued Henry. "I was exhausted from fighting that muskrat for so long and you two guys crawled back onto the middle seat after I said it was all clear. The two flashlights were still shining and lying on the bottom of the boat. We all pondered what had happened and decided then and there that daytime fishing was our game plan from then on. To this date, I don't believe any of us has ever fished at night." They all nodded in agreement. "When we got home, we all told our dads that the fish weren't biting."

After several minutes of silence, while we pondered the story, one of them finally said, "Remember Halloween?

"There were several of them," was the reply. "Halloween was the night to howl and we could get away with a lot—probably got away with more than what we should, but never with any real harm done."

"Yah," agreed another. "We were going around trick-or-treating like kids do, and one of us had firecrackers. Of course, he had some of his mom's matches and we were walking down the road by the town's water tower and lit one of those firecrackers and threw it out and it kind of landed near the edge of the road—BANG!—that was great."

"And we kept walking on down the road and one of us turned around and looked back and saw the firecracker had started a fire in the dry grass on the roadside."

"Oh, my gosh! And we ran back and started stomping at the burning grass until we finally put the fire out. That fire started in a hurry and had gotten three feet in diameter.

We hung around that spot for a while to make sure the fire didn't restart and decided that we had better be careful where we threw our firecrackers. I don't believe we lit any more that night."

"Remember that Halloween when we had some cat gut that my dad had in the barn for stitching stuff up, and we took some of that cat gut and tied it on a nail, and out in the woods we got some pitch pine off a pine tree. You know, that sticky stuff. And each of us had a string tied to a nail and a glob of pitch pine that we had let dry and harden and we would go from house to house.

"Back then, window glass wasn't always tight in its frame because the glazing putty would dry up and fall off the window, leaving the glass loose. Anyway, we would go to a house, sneak up to a window, and push the nail under the bottom of the window frame and take that rosin and rub it back and forth on the cat gut. That would make the glass rattle something fierce. And, you get two guys doing it, those windows would make the strangest noise you ever heard. We didn't know what it sounded like inside the house, but it made a horrible sound outside."

"Yeah, we'd quick jerk the nail out and run over and hide behind some bushes and out would come the people looking up and down their yard wondering what in the world was going on."

"I don't think they ever got wise to it. We went through the whole town that night. I don't think we missed anybody's house—we got 'em all. That was better than soaping windows, which if we got caught, our parents would have us cleaning everyone's windows in town. Yah, that was a lot of fun back then."

"We were seven or eight back then, and we were on our own at Halloween. Today, parents escort kids that age and don't let them get out of sight for fear the kids might get lost or hurt. They aren't streetwise at all like we were."

"Do you remember good, old Andy? We got to tell you about Andy. Andy was as strong as an ox—even when he was a kid. He had a hard time in school with certain subjects, but he was really good at math and doing things with his hands. The biggest thing going for him was solving problems of all kinds. He was so happy-go-lucky and always had a positive attitude on everything. We could never get him mad. If we had a problem that needed solving, we'd ask Andy, and in minutes he would have a solution for us."

"Andy's mother had a thing about Andy keeping his feet dry and made him wear boots over his shoes every day to school. One day during recess, we filled one of his boots almost to the top with water and stood it up next to his other boot. Now, Andy had a habit of slamming his feet into his boots without picking them up. We were going to have fun with him this day. We then went outside and played as innocent as we could, trying hard not to laugh at what was going to happen.

"Finally, at the end of the day, the teacher dismissed school and Andy ran over to his boots. He had to wear them home or he would catch the devil from his mom when he got home. He slammed his shoe into the empty boot and slammed his foot into the other boot and the water squirted clear up to the crotch of his pants. What a mess!

"In consternation, he removed the boot and dumped the remaining water on the floor and slammed his shoe back in the boot. He knew that somebody was having fun at his expense and he kind of laughed and noticed we four were watching his every move. He looked at us and said, 'One of these days, I'm going to even the score.' He got his books and headed on home.

"Andy always got up early with his dad to help milk the cows and feed the hogs and sheep before breakfast. He did the same every evening. He'd help his mother do most anything; especially if it was carrying something heavy, like filling washtubs with water. His mother had some chickens and sold eggs to mean, old Mr. Simpson, the owner of Simpson's General Store. Mr. Simpson wouldn't pay her the same price for her brown eggs as he did for the white ones and it always irked her as eggs were eggs regardless of the color of the shell.

"One day, it must have been a Saturday, Andy's mother was sick in bed so she asked Andy if he would take her eggs to Mr. Simpson and sell them. He said sure. He looked into the basket and saw she had put two dozen eggs inside and covered them with a napkin. Andy picked up the basket and carefully carried the eggs to Mr. Simpson's store. That's when I saw Andy and asked him what he was doing. He replied that he was going to Mr. Simpson's to sell him his mom's eggs. I asked him if I could tag along and he said sure.

"We went into the store and I went over to the candy case to study the candy and figure out what was the best buy. Andy went over to the checkout counter, lifted the basket of eggs up high, and carefully sat the basket on the counter. Mr. Simpson gruffly asked Andy what he wanted and Andy said that his mother was sick and that he was selling her eggs for her. Mr. Simpson lifted the napkin off the eggs and grumbled, 'More brown eggs.'

"Andy told him there were two dozen in the basket and that none of them was broken. Mr. Simpson must not have believed Andy because he removed each egg one at a time, examined it, and placed it in a shallow box on the counter. When he had finished, Andy asked him if they were all okay. Mr. Simpson nodded yes. He then went to his cash drawer and took out some money. Andy had overheard his mom explaining to his dad the wholesale price of white and brown eggs, so he knew how much he should be paid. Mr. Simpson placed the money in front of Andy and took the eggs over to another counter. Andy counted the money, but left it on the counter.

"When Mr. Simpson saw that Andy was still standing at the counter, with the money still in front of him, he gruffly asked Andy what was the matter. Andy looked Mr. Simpson straight in the eye and said, 'Eggs is eggs and brown eggs were just as good as white eggs.' Mr. Simpson replied that most everybody preferred white eggs to brown and that they would pay more for white ones. Andy had heard his dad once say the word *hogwash* and his mom hadn't complained; so Andy said, 'Hogwash.' Mr. Simpson said, 'There is your payment. Now, get along with you.'

"Andy replied, 'I don't like you cheating my mom,' to which Mr. Simpson said, 'Then take the eggs back home and eat them yourself.'

"'Mr. Simpson,' Andy replied, 'I don't like doing things to people behind their back; so I'm telling you I'm going to be your competition from now on unless you pay me the same price that you pay for white ones.'

"Mr. Simpson went over and got the box of brown eggs that were Andy's and set them on the counter next to the basket. Andy said, 'Please transfer my eggs back into my basket. I'm too short to do it.'

"Mr. Simpson grudgingly transferred the eggs back into the basket and told Andy to get out of his store. I wondered what Andy's mother was going to say about the unsold eggs. Andy motioned for me to come along with him and we left with the basket of unsold eggs. I asked him what he was going to tell his mom. 'I got a plan,' he said. 'Follow me.'

"When Andy had a plan, us kids knew it was always well thought out and he would have worked out in his mind how to carry out the plan to a successful conclusion. Andy headed down the street and turned right onto a side road, me tagging along. I asked him where we were going and he said to one of his mom's friends down the street. He turned onto a sidewalk leading to a house. When he got to the door, he knocked. A lady answered and said, 'Hi, Andy. What can I do for you?'

"He told her that Mr. Simpson was cheating his mom on the price for her eggs because they were brown. That eggs were eggs unless they were Amish eggs and his mom's eggs were Amish. The lady asked Andy how he knew that, and he answered that a few years back an Amish wagon train was passing through on their way westward and his mom saw them and hailed them down. They had livestock and cages with chickens. 'Mom asked if they would sell her two hens and a rooster. After some dickering, they came to terms at $5.00 for three chickens. She told the Amish man to pick out two good laying hens and a proud rooster while she cleared out our old chicken coop.

"'Mom and I started throwing stuff out of the coop, then she went inside the house and got $5.00 and closed the deal. That's how Mom got Amish chickens. And Mom propagated the chickens, and we now have twenty-four hens and a rooster we call George.'

"'And?' asked the lady.

"Andy explained that Mr. Simpson wasn't fair; so he told Mr. Simpson he was going into competition against him. 'I'm here to ask if you would like to buy eggs from Mom because they are fresh every day and they are special because they are Amish. Also the price would be better than Mr. Simpson's. And, as a friend, wouldn't you like to help Mom out?'

"The lady said she would be very happy to do so and

that she would also call her neighbors and friends to do likewise. Andy thanked her for the free advertising and asked if she needed any eggs today. She asked how many eggs he had. Andy said twenty-four and she said she'd buy six so he had some to sell to the neighbors. She paid Andy and picked out six eggs, put them in her bowl, and told Andy to go next door and wait while she called her neighbor.

"Andy said, 'Okay. I will make daily deliveries. If you need more eggs, just call Mom and place your order. Weekdays I can't deliver until school is out.' After thanking her again, we went next door. I didn't know anything about Amish chickens, but the lady did and her eyes lit up when Andy mentioned Amish. Three more stops and the twenty-four eggs were sold. Apparently these women didn't think much of Mr. Simpson and his cheap way of dealing.

"When Andy got home, he went to his mom and told her what he had done and that they were in business selling direct at a better price than selling wholesale to Mr. Simpson. He then asked if they could become partners in the enterprise, each sharing equally in the profits after paying expenses for feed. He said he would help her with caring for the chickens and he would do the deliveries. He held out his hand and asked, 'Is it a deal?' She shook his hand and started crying. A very young kid going into business was unheard of.

"Andy returned to the kitchen and started making a list of what he thought would be necessary to operate an enterprise, like sales receipts, ledgers, cashbox, etc. He returned to his mother and they went over the list, adding a few things that she thought of. Then Andy said, 'We need more chickens if we're going to really succeed. A few hens can sit on the eggs while I build us an incubator and get it set up.' His mom said, 'Andy, you're the best son any family could have. I love you so much.'

"Andy nosed around town and found someone who had an incubator. He studied it over, carefully making notes in his little notepad, and then he gathered everything necessary to make one. He used lots of scraps he salvaged from the dump and businesses around town. Within two weeks, he had an incubator built.

"After the incubator was working, Andy became serious when he wasn't talking with someone, almost like he was mad. But the truth was, he was in deep thought. He would draw a few lines on a piece of paper and write a few notes in his pocket notebook. Then he'd go out to the barn, and return with a sad expression on his face. Again he would draw more lines on the paper; it looked like a design of something, then he would do more line drawings, showing an end view of the first design. He was going to build something. After he made a list of materials, he went to his mom and told her he was leaving the house for a little while and would be back in time for chores.

"A little while later, he returned with a beaming smile. He went to his mom and said they had to have a business meeting. She put down her knitting and listened. Andy told her he had a project for the egg business and needed to withdraw $25 from the profits. She asked what for and he replied it was a secret surprise for her. She answered that he always knew what he was doing and she trusted in his good judgment. 'Use whatever funds you need, and thank you for telling me in advance.'

"Andy went to the phone, dialed a number, and told the person on the other end to carry out the material plan. The next day, the town's lumber truck pulled into the driveway and Andy helped the man unload some lumber and a bag of something. What Andy made, with help from his dad, was a feed bin for the chickens—a five-foot long, gravity-flow bin with two big compartments and a smaller section in between them. Andy explained to his mother that he'd refill the bins when low on food and the feed would no longer be on the floor. Once again, Andy's parents were proud of their son and his ingenuity."

After listening to this memory of Andy, another guy decided to share one of his. "One early fall day, the five of us were sauntering through town when Andy said, 'How about we get some apples to eat?' We all knew Andy had come up with a great idea—but where could we snitch some free apples? Andy said, 'We are going to people who will give us enough apples so we can eat some and plenty more for our moms so they can make fresh apple pies.' We knew then that Andy had come up with another great plan: apples for the taking.

"Andy liked to put us off when he had something in mind. He would lead us like sheep to wherever he was going. We followed him a few blocks and turned onto a side street and walked up to the porch where Mr. and Mrs. Farnham were sitting. After exchanging hellos, Andy asked Mr. Farnham why he hadn't picked his apples. Mr. Farnham replied that he was too feeble to climb the picking ladder so he had to wait until they dropped to the ground. Andy had an idea that Mrs. Farnham wouldn't let him climb the ladder because of its condition—Andy had looked over the picking ladder and it was way too dangerous to use. Andy said that the five of us would pick what we could reach, providing we could have some apples to take home to our moms to make pies. The Farnhams looked at each other and Mrs. Farnham said it was a deal and we would find some baskets in the back shed.

"We got five baskets, one for each of us, and we all started picking apples as high as we could reach. We filled two baskets to the top and Mr. Farnham told us we had done a great job. Andy said we weren't done yet; that there were more apples to pick. The four of us told Andy we couldn't reach any higher. 'But two of us can,' he countered.

"Remember, Andy was a very strong boy and he proved it to us that afternoon. He said we were going to pick apples higher up and that three of us were to catch apples as they were tossed down and put them in a basket. Andy was just under the tree branches when he called for one of us to climb onto his shoulders. I did and Andy stood up straight like I wasn't even on him and walked so I could reach the higher apples. We filled the three remaining baskets and brought two more out from the shed. We filled one of the baskets and about three quarters of the last one, leaving only a few apples at the very top of the tree. Andy had held us on his shoulders for an hour, with a break every ten to fifteen minutes to stretch his legs. His brute strength had saved the day.

"As we picked those last apples, Mrs. Farnham had gone into the house and returned with five grocery bags. She and her husband filled the five bags not quite full so the apples wouldn't spill out. She asked if we would carry the remaining baskets to the shed and that the five bags of apples were for our mothers to use. We thanked them and waved goodbye as we headed home, with each of us eating a freshly picked apple.

"Andy would make a fair offer of a deal—and everybody came out a winner."

Chapter 8

"IT SOUNDS LIKE ALL OF YOU LIKED ANDY A LOT," I said. "But he isn't here. Did he move away?"

Three of the guys looked at Henry, who said, "I guess it's my turn to tell a story. It may take some time, though."

I said I had lots of time; so Henry began.

"Andy and I were both eighteen and had taken our physicals for the draft. We were drafted at the same time and shipped to Fort Benning, Georgia, for basic training. The Army has the habit of sending the guys from the South to northern forts and those who are from the North are sent to the South. That's how we ended up at Fort Benning for infantry training.

"Andy and I were assigned to the same squad and we really became close to each other. Andy, for whatever reason, became stronger than almost any two guys together, and no matter how hard they drove us, Andy never got tired. In part of our training, we were taught how to fire rifles and to maintain them under any condition. Both of us passed gunnery as sharpshooters, the highest rating, but somehow Andy convinced our CO that he wanted to try out the thirty-caliber machine gun.

"The CO asked why the machine gun, and Andy had

replied jokingly that he was good with things that had lots of parts and the machine gun had more parts than a rifle. A machine gunner had to have an ammo feeder and Andy requested me for that job. The CO, company Sergeant, Andy, and I went to the gunnery range with two cases of ammo and a thirty-caliber machine gun. We learned later that the CO had never had anybody request a machine gun as a weapon of choice. He wanted to see what kind of nut he had in his company.

"We arrived at the gunnery range and the Sergeant started instructing us on the operation of the gun. Andy, as usual, was very intent on everything the Sergeant said and asked the Sergeant to open up the breach. He wanted to see what was inside and how the parts worked. This was also a new question for the CO, usually a recruit wanted to fire the gun first and learn about it later. The Sergeant obliged and the Captain stood by, watching closely. That having been done, Andy and I were shown how to set up the gun and feed the ammo belt, etc. The Sergeant had us set up the gun in firing position and aimed the gun toward the target. Andy got into position, set the gun up to fire single shots, not automatic, and the Sergeant asked Andy why he did that. Andy replied he wanted to know how much elevation would be needed to hit the target, how much wind drift there was, and how the gun would feel to him when fired.

"The Sergeant looked over to the Captain and each thought to himself that this young kid was asking the right questions and giving the right answers to questions. If he could do as well in the firing of the gun, they would have the perfect soldier for the task. The Sergeant told Andy to commence firing. The first shot hit about twenty-five feet in front of the target and slightly to one side. The second shot was in line with the bull's-eye and the third hit the bull's-eye dead center. The Sergeant then told Andy to fire three rounds on automatic, which Andy did. Three rounds hit the bull's-eye at 100 yards. The Sergeant told Andy to fire five rounds on automatic, which Andy did and hit the bull's-eye five more times.

"The Captain was pleased because he had never seen a recruit take to a machine gun so fast, and with apparent dead accuracy. When he told Andy he'd done a great job, Andy replied that what he knew of fighting in battle was that the enemy didn't stand still like a target. He would need experience at a moving target. The Captain asked Andy if he was sure he wanted to carry a machine gun because it was four times heavier than a rifle. Andy said yes. He would train himself to carry the extra weight and the machine gun was his weapon of choice as long as Henry was his ammo man. The Sergeant told Andy to unload the gun. Andy looked to see if the bullet chamber was empty and there was a bullet in the chamber. He removed the bullet and gave it to me to reinstall in the gun belt.

"The Captain asked if we had known each other before being drafted. We replied that we had been buddies all of our lives and we didn't want to be separated, ever. Andy picked up the machine gun and, with one hand, carried it back to the jeep. The next day's schedule was a twenty-mile hike with full sixty-pound packs. It was going to be a grueling march. Andy asked the Sergeant to get him a manual for the machine gun and he also wanted a cleaning kit. Andy said he'd like to keep the gun so he could study it and get accustomed to carrying it. The Captain said he couldn't keep it in the barracks, it would have to be returned to the armory. After Andy was assigned to a regular unit, it could be possible to keep one in his possession. Andy said he guessed he'd have to spend his time off in the armory.

"About that time, the Korean War had started and our company was ordered for active duty in Korea. Green troops in a war zone. Andy and I were still together. Andy now had his machine gun with him all the time. He'd taught himself to disassemble and reassemble the machine gun in total darkness. He would disassemble the mechanism and begin working on all the parts with his private assortment of sandpaper and tools. He carried his pocket magnifier and looked at every part and how it meshed with an adjacent part. He then moved them against each other until their action was to his general satisfaction, but not perfect. He even ordered six replacement parts even though the gun seemed to work fine. I asked why he was getting several of each part; his answer was simply that mass-produced parts had plus or minus tolerances and no two were exactly alike. He'd assemble the weapon with a combination and check for smoothness of operation and shake the weapon for rattling. If that combination failed his standard, he'd try a different set and test again. He spent hours doing this.

"When I asked him for a better explanation, he said: 'You have seen auto engines that were noisy or didn't perform as well as others. Sometimes one engine will outperform all of the others and machine guns are no different. Some combination together made for poor performance, others would do much better.' When he was on the front line, Andy wanted the very best performance from his machine gun. "The better the match of parts, the better performance and a lesser chance of the gun jamming. The last thing he wanted was a gun to jam when under attack and lives were at stake. He had brought his calipers from home and had measured every single part in his assortment and had marked each in such a way that he could identify it from the others. The specs for each part were written in his pocket notebook and he could match up various sets that could work well together in his weapon.

"He asked the Captain if he could have a case of ammo

and permission to test fire the gun in a safe area. The Captain wanted to know why. Andy told him what he had been doing and wanted to be sure the weapon performed to his satisfaction. The Captain nodded and told Andy where and when he could test fire and that he and the Sergeant would come along. We all went to an approved area, set up some targets, and started test firing. The Sergeant immediately commented that Andy's machine gun sounded different. It wasn't as loud nor did it chatter like machine guns exactly like Andy's. The Captain had Andy fire off some more rounds of ammo and agreed with the Sergeant that this gun was a super performer. When we returned to base camp, Andy cleaned his weapon and boxed all of the extra parts in a small box.

"While we were on a break, we went to Division Headquarters and Andy asked a Sergeant if he could see the Commanding General. The Sergeant informed us that Privates don't converse with generals and to get lost. Andy told the Sergeant that it was concerning the battles and that exceptions should be made to the rule and that Privates can have something of value that Generals ought to hear. The Sergeant finally gave up and told us to have a seat. It was Andy's neck in a noose, he said. And Andy would likely spend time in the jug or be court martialed. Andy said he'd rather have that than have more G I get killed.

"We waited all morning, quietly sitting off to one side while watching officers with lots of papers come and go from the General's office. About 1:30 the Commanding General came out of his office and Andy and I jumped to attention and saluted him. The General continued walking, then stopped, and addressed the Desk Sergeant. 'Why are these two privates sitting in my outer office?' The Sergeant answered, 'We wouldn't tell him—only that more soldiers were going to get killed needlessly if you didn't hear them out, Sir.' The General whirled around, came up to us, and asked what was so damn important that we'd risk court martial just to tell him something.

"Andy identified us and our Unit then said that the Army was using the wrong type of artillery in support of the infantry. Andy explained that the North Koreans were no dummies and would hole up in the valley in front of our hill position and the 75 mm would shoot over their heads and hit the opposite hillside from us, where there were no enemy troops. He said he tried protocol and no help came. 'I have sent to your attention five letters explaining this situation and that we needed howitzers instead of field artillery. Nothing has happened to improve the situation and guys are getting killed because of it. If you want to court martial us, do so, but get some howitzers up there fast. We go back to the front tomorrow and this was the only way to be sure you got the message.'

The general whirled around and in a loud voice said, 'Does anybody know about these five letters sent to me?' A Major answered that he had read the letters and figured it was from a dumb nut that wanted off the front lines. The general yelled again. 'If any more letters come to me with such battle information, I want to know at once! And now I know why we are having a devil of a time making headway in this war. Cut immediate orders to supply that we get every available howitzer in Korea, Japan, and the United States. One thousand will do for a start.' The General turned to us and said he was making us Sergeants effective immediately. He wished us luck on the front, saluted us, and strode away.

"The office began to buzz with vigorous activity and the Desk Sergeant told Andy and me to wait because he was cutting orders for our promotions to Staff Sergeant per the General's orders. He thanked us, shook our hands, and said, 'Thank goodness you guys had the guts to act" and then handed us papers promoting us to Staff Sergeant.

"The next day we returned to the front to resume the battle, on a hill that the Army had assigned a number. We were brought up to support, not relieve, any troops and knew something was up. The soldiers we joined told us that that hill had changed hands two times already and the enemy wanted to take and hold it in the worst way. Andy and I then knew we were soon going to be in for a battle. That night we could hear a lot of noise down in the valley in front of us. They had built up a larger force of troops and at dawn our position was going to be under heavy attack.

"The attack came as we had expected. With dawn, we could see over 1,000 enemy soldiers charging toward our position. Our mortars started lobbing shells at them and they still kept coming. When they came in range, we started firing our weapons. We were inflicting heavy losses to them but they still kept charging us. Suddenly two of our Navy fighters swooped down on them and fired all of their rockets into the charging enemy, strafed them over and over until they left, probably using up all their ammo. The enemy fell back and all was quiet the rest of the day, but that night more activity was heard in the valley below and we knew the next morning their charge on us would begin again.

"That night we set off flares over the valley. The valley was swarming with many more soldiers than the day before. And, as before, we had the wrong artillery to bombard them, no howitzers yet. During the night, heavy fog had settled into the valley below and although we were higher up, our hilltop position had us in light fog also. That was not going to be good because the enemy would be much closer before we would be able to see them. Also there would be no air cover support because of the fog.

"Most of us couldn't sleep. We were too keyed up; so, we just rested. At dawn, the onslaught hit us with both sides firing with everything they had. Andy shot up four boxes of ammo. It began to rain and when the raindrops hit the barrel of his thirty-caliber, the water turned to steam. His gun had been working perfectly, but with such heavy firing in such a short time, the barrel was sure to melt down.

"Then another mad charge hit and both sides were shooting at each other as before. We could hear screams of agony from our men, even over the roar of the gunfire. Suddenly a torrential downpour dumped on everybody. The shooting stopped and orders came to fall back at once. I had been hit by shrapnel in the back and blood was now soaking through my clothing. Everybody gathered up their stuff and we were forming up for an orderly withdrawal, except Andy. I told him, 'Come on, guy. We have to get out of here, now.' He noticed my blood and yelled, 'Medic!' I told him I was okay and could walk back. 'Get going,' he said. He was going to cover our withdrawal as long as possible and when the ammo ran out, he would run like hell to catch up with us. The rain let up and Andy's gun started firing again, on and on. The enemy was charging the hill again. We heard the pop of a grenade and all went silent. I knew Andy had fought until his last breath so we could withdraw safely. In withdrawal, all dead and wounded are taken back; so nobody but Andy had remained. Our losses were heavy, but in no way compared to the hundreds of losses the enemy had.

"I heard later that sixteen howitzers had arrived on scene that afternoon but had been delayed because of the fog. They had been scheduled to be onsite before dawn. Once they were in position, they and the artillery, blasted that hill and valley for five hours straight. There wasn't a living person to be found. That hill, valley, and the slope of the hill was one giant shell hole.

"The doctors at the M.A.S.H. unit removed the shrapnel from my back and I was going home without my best buddy. Our unit commander put in an order for the Silver Star award for Andy. I was sitting on my bunk, waiting to be evacuated to the rear, when suddenly the Commanding General stepped into our tent. I recognized him immediately, stood up, and came to a smart attention and saluted him. He returned the salute, then recognized me, and came over to me. He asked where Andy was. I told him what Andy had done for all his buddies and how Andy had made that thirty-caliber machine gun the most perfect weapon in the Army. The General said he would send out a team to search the hilltop and try to retrieve the weapon. I added that Andy had the letter "A" scratched on the trigger guard for identification, and his .45 sidearm also. The General told his orderly to take my name, home address, and unit number before moving on to visit with the other wounded in the tent.

"The army sent me to Japan for recovery, then to Fort Benning for final treatment and discharge from the Army. Just before my discharge, I received a personal letter on the General's stationery stating that his search team had found Andy's machine gun. There were only ten rounds of ammo left in the gun belt, fourteen empty ammo cases, and the gun barrel was burned out beyond any further use. He stated that the gun had been shipped to Army Ordnance for complete evaluation, paying particular attention to the breach mechanism and that it would be displayed as an historic weapon. He also said that in getting Andy's duffel bag, they found all of his notes and drawings on his machine gun; they too were being returned with the gun to Ordnance.

"After the arrival of the Howitzers, the fighting in Korea started to change. Before long, every battalion had at least two batteries of Howitzers and with the 75 mm artillery, they would blanket the hills and valleys with exploding shells that literally started to take the fight out of the North Korean soldiers. Thousands were either killed or wounded, and when shells started exploding around them, they would throw down their weapons and run to their rear where the big guns kept on blanketing the area. The tide of the war changed and the enemy retreated almost to the 38th Parallel when a ceasefire was declared."

I realized the storytelling was over. I told Henry that with him telling the story he had kept to himself for all these years, maybe he could finally have closure. He nodded yes.

I said my goodbyes to them and Maggie, and slowly walked to the entrance. Once I was outside, I decided a final walk through town would be a fitting tribute to Andy, a hero I never knew.

Chapter 9

I HEADED NORTH, AIMING FOR US-2. MY PLAN WAS to stop in Ashland, Wisconsin. The AAA tour book said it is one of the ports where iron-ore ingots are loaded onto ships. I thought Ashland would be a good place to take a look at the harbor and see how many ships are docked for the winter.

Duluth is also known for shipping iron ore, but since Ashland is a much smaller city and less commercialized, it will be easier for me to get around there. Also, Ashland's downtown is known for twelve murals painted on some of its early-twentieth-century buildings.

When I arrived, the town was bustling with winter sports activity. I saw many SUVs and vans with skies, snowboards, and snowshoes strapped to them. I took some pictures of the murals and stopped in most of the shops in that part of town. I'm sure the people who live in northern Wisconsin and northwestern Minnesota are aware of this city of only 8,000 people. Being from Michigan, I had never heard of Ashland. It seemed like it would be a wonderful place to reside because of all the things you can do there. The store people were very friendly and always willing to be helpful if I had a question. I decided to bypass Duluth and continue west into Minnesota.

At Duluth, I picked up the junction of I-35 and headed south until I would junction with M-23 and take the less-traveled route to I-90. There would be more things to see and small towns to visit, with less confusion, then the all-Interstate route on the TripTik. Plus I would avoid Minneapolis completely.

In one of the towns off M-23, I pulled in to gas up. I asked the gas station attendant if they always had this much snow. "Oh, no," she said. "We got hammered yesterday with twenty-four inches of this wet stuff, which is rare for here. Moist air came in from the southwest and it got slammed into by an Arctic blast from Canada.

"The town is trying to dig itself out today. Sam's Excavating was here at five o'clock this morning, plowing out my driveway to the gas pumps; otherwise we wouldn't be open for business. That's him and his ten-year old son across the street plowing out the restaurant."

While filling my gas tank, I saw a tandem-wheel truck come into the parking lot and a small boy get out of that big end loader and run into the restaurant. I would say the end loader had to be at least a ten-yarder and it was being operated by a ten-year-old. The boy came out, jumped into the loader, wheeled it into a big snow pile, filled the bucket, backed away, and swung it around and dumped the load into the truck. Every move he made was picture perfect.

I asked the attendant if I could park Susie off to the side while I had a cup of coffee and a doughnut. She said yes, and the doughnuts were leftovers.

M-23 had been plowed; so I walked across the street to the restaurant and stood off to the side to watch the young boy operate the end loader. This kid was good. His dad came back after dumping his load and the boy started filling the dump truck again without any wasted motion.

The father stepped out of his truck and walked over to me and asked if he could help me with something. I told him I was enjoying watching his son operate the loader. "I bet he's better than anybody you could hire," I said.

He said, "Yep! He started riding shotgun with me last year and he begged me so much to learn to operate it, I gave in and taught him. He took right to it. When he isn't in school, we work as a team. I pay him full wages and he banks his earnings to save up for college. Can you imagine that?!"

I told him, "Yes, I could, because I knew another boy who was almost like his son." Of course, I was thinking of Andy.

The man's cell phone rang and he answered it. Another request to plow a driveway. He ended the call and excused himself. "Got to get back to work," he said. "Nice meeting." He returned to his truck and drove off with another load of snow.

Chapter 10

I CLIMBED INTO SUSIE AND HEADED SOUTHWEST FOR more unknown stops. When I arrived at the junction with I-90, I proceeded west to Mitchell, South Dakota. Most people have never heard of Mitchell—except pheasant hunters. If given a chance to hunt there any fall, they would welcome it. There are hundreds of acres of prairie corn stubble infested with these pheasants. And downtown Mitchell has the world's only Corn Palace that is decorated each year with corn.

I located the Dakota Discovery Center at the college and spent half a day browsing through it. Beautiful Native American beadwork and quilts, and all sorts of historical items that had been collected over decades, were on display there. I couldn't get anybody to tell me their stories so I decided to drive toward Rapid City.

On the eastern side of Rapid City, I stopped at the Visitors Center for brochures on Hot Springs, South Dakota, and the Mammoth Site. That afternoon, I got on Highway 79 and headed south toward Hot Springs, and enjoyed the picturesque landscape along the way.

I found the Chamber of Commerce office, stepped inside,

and approached an attendant. "What attractions, including the Mammoth Site, would be of interest in the area?" I asked. The woman loaded me up with all sorts of information, including a map of the region and brochures on places she thought would be of interest. She also suggested a bed and breakfast. I asked her to call them and ask if they had an opening and how much it would cost. She got right on the phone and said they had a bedroom available. When she told me the price, I told her I would take it for two nights. I thanked the lady and left to check in at the B & B.

After I registered for the room, a woman showed me to my room. It was nicely decorated; light and cheery. I told her I was going downtown to get my evening dinner and would be back later.

I found a home-style restaurant and stepped inside. It was about 4:30 so it was quiet, with only a few diners. A lady asked where I would like to sit. I noticed an older man sitting alone at a table. I told the woman that if he would like some company, I would join him. She asked the man and he said sure.

The lady introduced the man as Harold. I responded with my name, sat down, and we started conversing. I told him about myself, where I was from, and why I was passing through Rapid City. He then started to narrate his life.

He had lived in this area all of his life. After serving in the military in Korea, he came home and couldn't find a job. "My father said that if I would run a country general store at his house, he would put a store addition to the front of the house and I could live with them. I could learn how to run the business and, with my folks' help and training, I could have a great place to live and work. The addition was built and a refrigeration-cooler unit was purchased and installed. I built all of the display cabinets for the merchandise we would carry.

"I had been dating my high school sweetheart during the construction of the addition, and not long after the store was up and running we got married. We lived with my parents.

"We carried all of the essential food items, fresh meat, the daily newspaper from Rapid City, and we had two gas pumps out front. From the first day we opened, the business was a success. The newspapers really helped, even though we didn't make much of a profit on them. They got people to come into the store every day.

"My folks died and my wife and I inherited the business and property. A few years back, my wife's health started to fail and we were forced to sell the business so she would be closer to her doctors. She passed away about three years ago. I now live alone, down the street. I don't do much of anything anymore except watch TV, eat, and sleep. I don't have any desire to travel alone."

It was quiet between us for a bit; then I asked him if he had known any interesting people that had lived in the area. He sat quietly, occasionally rubbing his fingers around his coffee cup, not saying a word. I thought maybe he hadn't heard me and was about to ask him again when he spoke up. "Yes, there were four people that were very unusual; they being Rudolph, Kate and Jake, and Herman." He then told me about them.

"Rudolph was a big man. Six two or three, with whiskers all over his face, but neatly trimmed. He would get to know other people in the area by coming to our store frequently for food, but never buying a newspaper. He would talk to people in the store with a strong German accent and, if someone pulled into his driveway that he didn't recognize, he would beat a trail out the back door of his house and vanish into the woods. If there was a lady in the auto, he might hang around and ask what they wanted. He didn't own a car, so he walked everywhere he went.

"After a number of years, the story came out that Rudolph was a deserter from the Prussian Army in World War I. Somehow he had gotten to the U.S. and had walked across the country until he settled here. He was especially afraid of men because he thought they were Germans coming to take him back to Germany and prison, or that they were from the Immigration Bureau to deport him because he had no papers allowing him to be here.

"He walked every inch of the woods for miles around and stumbled on a headstone marking a grave for a little girl and a smaller stone for her brother. Very few people knew of this gravesite, and those who did kept it a secret. Each spring Rudolph would pick wildflowers and take them to that gravesite, brush away the leaves, pull the weeds, and clean up the area. There was a large fallen tree close by and he would sit there for long periods of time, I guess thinking of his family back in Germany and how he missed them. To my knowledge, he never had any contact with them. "He died some thirty years or so ago. Everyone who knew him, took up a collection and purchased a headstone for him. Rudolph is buried in the little township cemetery.

"A few years after Rudolph died, a family who knew him purchased a parcel of land near his home and built some horse stables and a barn and started a riding stable. They had horses that they rented and stalls so people could stable their horses there for a fee. There are numerous two-track trails winding around the forest and open areas. The business was successful and horsemen and their families would come from quite a distance to spend time in this beautiful area. The owners named the business Ranch Rudolph; so his name lives on."

What a sad story, I thought. And all brought on by war. While I was still reflecting on Rudolph's life, Harold started to tell me about Kate and Jake.

"When Kate was young, she had been a nurse, maybe in the military—we never really knew. She walked away from that career and settled on a parcel of land on a gravel road in the forest. Her appearance was terrible. She had long, stringy hair with a woolen stocking cap pulled down, covering her ears. She wore an old army trench coat and worn hunting boots that she never polished. She lived in a burned out house trailer, of which the whole front half was missing. Like Rudolph, Kate walked wherever she went—but would hardly speak to anyone, including my wife and me.

"Kate had hung a heavy blanket over the open end of the trailer and slept in the rear portion, which was apparently the bedroom and a tiny bathroom. She had an old, wood-burning stove outside that she used year-round to cook her meals on and heat water. She had the area picked clean of any dead sticks, branches, and any wood she could burn. She did have an ax that she used on the bigger timber.

"Usually when she came to the store to buy food, she would eye the meat case and then order what she wanted. But she always wanted fresh meat from my back freezer and not meat from the display case. Of all her sloppy ways, Kate was very particular on the meat she bought.

"Nobody knows how it came about, but one day, another half-burnt trailer was put next to hers and a guy named Jake showed up. They both lived there for many years, each using their own trailer. They did come into my store together, with very few words being spoken between them.

"Eventually, they both disappeared and both of the trailers were hauled away. Nobody ever knew what became of them."

"Fascinating," I said. And, before I could say more, Harold went on with the third man.

"Now, Herman the Hermit was a very nice man. He was always friendly," began Harold. "The way he lived was different. He had dug out a chunk of steep hillside and erected a dwelling into the hill with a doorway extending outside. He had a wood cook stove inside, with a chimney that extended through the roof. He covered the roof with dirt and sod. This is the where he lived until his death.

"The only time anybody saw Herman was when he came to our store or did odd jobs for people in the area. When he got a job, he worked hard, without any breaks or slowing down on his task. Those jobs helped him keep food on his table, although he patrolled the busier highways each night looking for roadkill. He would draw a circle around the roadkill with chalk, then continue on down the road. The next morning, he would retrace his steps carrying a gunny sack. When he came upon roadkill that didn't have a chalk circle around it, he would put it in his sack. Animals without a circle were fresh kill, so in that way he always had fresh meat to eat.

"Some people would box fresh roadkill and give it to him. Herman would eat any animal, including deer, raccoons, rabbits, possum, and porcupines. He knew how to prepare and flavor these animals so they were good eating. Some he would cut into strips and make jerky. When he made a new batch of jerky, he would give me a few strips when he came to the store. I never could figure out what kind of animal it was from because it all tasted good and I never got sick from it."

By this time, the restaurant was getting busy. We decided we'd better leave and free up the table. When we were outside, I asked Harold if, rather than sitting alone the next day, he would like to ride shotgun with me tomorrow and direct me to points of interest in the Hot Springs area. He said yes. We agreed to meet at seven-thirty the next morning, at the restaurant for breakfast; then get on the road, he being my tour guide.

After breakfast, we headed for the Mammoth Site. It was very impressive. We toured the buildings and marveled at the size of the bones of the Colombian and Wooly Mammoths. There was one mammoth skeleton assembled in a building—it had to be as large as the largest whale.

This site was discovered in 1974, by accident. About 20,000 years ago, mammoths roamed the area. The theory is they were in search of water and found their way there. But the area was actually a giant sink hole; so when the large beasts went into the water for a drink, they couldn't get out because the sides of the hole were too slippery.

At last count, fifty-eight Colombian and three Wooly Mammoths have been dug up and extracted. Excavation continues today. If you want to dig, you can pay a $150 fee and dig for two weeks. A Google search for "Mammoth Site" will get you to their website and lots of information.

From there, Harold and I traveled north to Wind Cave National Park. The erosion caused by wind had created tunnels of all shapes and sizes. For me, it was another natural wonder of the world. After leaving that area, Harold took me on side roads and two-tracks through some wonderful areas seldom seen by vacationers. All that afternoon and the next day, he kept directing me on side excursions. He said he was glad Susie was a 4-wheel drive vehicle. Harold said that some trails were for hikers only and horseback was a bad idea. Sometimes he would point out a place for a side trip that we couldn't take because of trail washouts.

In those two days, Harold and I became close friends. Harold didn't have that sad-eyed look any longer. Our time together turned him around mentally and he told me he was going to plan something each day, and maybe hire himself out as a tourist guide. I told him that sounded like a great idea and he would have more fun than he had had in a long time.

After breakfast the next morning, we shook hands and wished each other well; agreeing to stay in touch. I then headed west to US-18. I was traveling to Cheyenne and then Laramie, Wyoming, to see my friends Ronda and Bob Boyd.

Chapter 11

I WAS HEADING SOUTH ON US-18 IN WYOMING WHEN I stopped in a small town called Lusk. Little did I know what was going to transpire in the next two hours.

I spotted a bakery and coffee shop on the main street and decided to take a break to stretch my legs. Sweets and coffee sounded good. Seated at a large table by himself was a white-haired gentleman, easily in his late eighties, sipping a cup of coffee. I asked if I could join him at the table. He said, "Sure. Have a seat."

"Life can get kind of dull once we hit eighty, if we don't get something going to occupy ourselves," I offered. He agreed. I asked him what he had done for a living. He replied that he was a farmer until he deeded his 1,200-acre farm and nursery to his married son and daughter.

"That's a pretty large farm," I said. "What did you grow or raise?" He thought for a minute and then started into a narrative I had not expected.

"My father and mother had a 160-acre farm in Michigan, northwest of Ann Arbor. I was drafted into the Army Corps of Engineers and sent to Fort Belvoir, Virginia in January 1945. V-E Day ended the war in Europe, and I never left Fort Belvoir. I served my two years there until my discharge.

"I enrolled at the University of Michigan that fall using the GI Bill. The professors were a pompous bunch of rascals and looked down their noses at any veterans who were in their classes. For the most part, they were a bunch of egotistical snobs that thought they were the ones who had won the war in Europe. I got through the first semester with a C average and decided that my father's livestock treated me better than the professors did; so I quit college and went to work for my parents on their farm.

"Everything was going fine, except my father didn't pay me a whole lot; so I joined the Air Force Reserves at Selfridge Air Force Base north of Detroit. Being a Staff Sergeant meant I would have a little more income to supplement my farm wages. That was working out pretty well, until the Korea War started and my Air Force Wing Unit was activated. I was ordered to report to Walker Air Force Base in Roswell, New Mexico, for duty.

"There I was, twenty-four years old, no serious girlfriend, and now going to spend another two years in the military, in a place 1,900 miles from home. For a few dollars a month, I was stuck there for at least two years. I was assigned to the Transportation Unit and my job was seeing to all freight coming and going from the air base. A primary job I had was scheduling all van moves for Airmen being transferred to the base or to Airmen being transferred to another base. The vans, of course, would carry the airmen's family household goods to their new assignment.

"Each day I would receive a roster of new transfers, and I would prepare the necessary paperwork and schedule the packing and pickup for each of the transfers so each van was fully packed and ready to go. Now, the trick to doing this was to have one destination for the loaded trailer and then to have the trailer fully loaded on the return trip to New

Mexico. Every Air Base has an Airman, all Sergeants, doing the same job I was doing; so we would call each other and set up a full load for the return trip to New Mexico.

"For the most part, the van company I used was Red Ball Van Lines. They realized how good of a job I was doing having their vans fully loaded both going and coming, and the van drivers would jump at the chance to deliver my shipments as they would get paid for full loads both ways.

"Soon after I was on the base, I met another Sergeant who was from Joliet, Illinois. We got to be close, and stayed friends for the rest of our lives. He was called "Red." Each day when Red and I got off duty, we drove taxicabs in Roswell for extra income, and to have something to do besides just sitting around.

"Because of my Air Force job, I knew when incoming personnel flights would be arriving, so both of us would be on hand to pick up passengers and take them to Roswell. We were both tired of living on base; so we devised a plan to live in a motel off the base—at no charge. If the plan worked, we would have it made.

"From driving taxies, we both knew which motels were always full and which ones were starving for lack of customers. We went to one of the starving motels and offered the owner a deal: if he would rent us a room with two double beds at no charge, we would have his motel filled to capacity within a few days.

"He balked at the no charge bit. We answered that we guessed he would then go bankrupt for lack of business. The word *bankrupt* hit home in a hurry and, reluctantly, he agreed to our plan. We could move into a unit at the far end of the motel the next evening. We said fine, and we wanted housekeeping just once a week not every day. The next evening, Red and I moved into our new quarters at the motel.

The plan worked perfectly for six months—his motel was almost always full—until one evening, the owner posted a note on our room door. He wanted us to go to the office to see him.

"When we stepped into the office, he was waiting for us. He told us he was losing rental on our room and he had to have 50 percent of the regular room rate so it wouldn't be a total loss to him. We told him that wasn't the deal but he refused to back down. We told him we would think it over and get back to him the following night.

That night, we immediately went to another starving motel and offered the same deal. Our offer was gratefully accepted. We could move in the next night. We never paid for lodging in Roswell.

"Later, when we told him that our discharge from the Air Force was coming up very soon, he regretted us leaving and told us we had saved his business from going under. We told him that some other airmen also drove taxicabs so we would pass the word on.

"Red was discharged five days ahead of me. We hated to part company and agreed to keep in touch. Four days before my discharge, a First Lieutenant barged into our transportation office and demanded to see the officer in charge. He was directed to me but he said I wasn't the officer in charge and that was who he was going to see. This Lieutenant was belligerent and nasty to me because I was only a lowly non-com. I told him that the Major was in a conference and I would notify the Major when he was free. Then I suggested he have a seat and a cup of coffee if he desired. He declined both offers and started pacing the floor.

"Twenty minutes later, the Major ended his call and I notified him that there was a First Lieutenant waiting to see him and he wouldn't tell me what the meeting was about.

The Major told me to let him into his office. I led the Lieutenant to the Major's office, opened the door, and the lieutenant charged into the office. I closed the door and returned to my desk only to be interrupted by the Major telling the Lieutenant that I handled all household van moves and he had to tell me the problem. The lieutenant bellowed at me that he had been transferred to Roswell and his family would be arriving shortly. He wanted his household goods in his assigned quarters now. I got his name and immediately searched my records of incoming papers for shipment—nothing was to be found. I tried to explain to him that probably because we had just come off a weekend, the paperwork had been delayed. I told him I would check the next morning's mail and look into the matter. He said, 'Don't you get an afternoon mail?' 'Not always,' I said. He made a nasty remark about me not knowing what I was doing, then said he would return in the afternoon.

"I quickly realized that this bird was going to put me down every chance he could. That afternoon, he came in again and started raising hell with me because I hadn't received anything about his household goods. The next morning, he was back again, and acted worse than he had the day before. I said I would call his former Air Base and find out what was happening.

"The paperwork didn't arrive that afternoon either, so I called my cohort in South Dakota to find out where the move stood. The Sergeant there said that he had unfriendly dealings with the Lieutenant about having his household goods shipped out first ahead of anybody else. Protocol calls for officers of higher rank to be taken care of first. For some reason, the orders for his move got placed on the bottom of the pile.

"There weren't enough moving vans available; so his

household furniture pickup was delayed a day. I laughed over the phone and made the comment that it didn't pay to mess with Sergeants. He laughed too and then said that the Lieutenant had insisted that his goods be loaded first—and so, his was the first on the van, which meant it would be the last off. Two of the other three deliveries were going elsewhere. . The Sergeant said the paperwork was in the mail and I should have it the next day. I thanked him for the wonderful job he had done, and told him I was being discharged in two days. No words were said between us about how the Lieutenant had been screwed and that both of us had happy smiles on our faces.

"That afternoon, the Lieutenant came charging into my office. After he raved at me for ten minutes, I told him his van was on the road, with three other deliveries before his, and it might arrive tomorrow, which I knew wouldn't happen. This knucklehead had me thoroughly aroused and I had a plan to fix him so good that he would never forget what was going to happen.

"The next day, I set about typing new waybills and a manifest on the Lieutenant's goods. I called the Sergeant on duty at the base's receiving warehouse and asked him to be looking for this particular shipment, to put it off to the side, away from all other shipments, and to call me the minute it arrived. He said he would do so. The lieutenant came in as expected that afternoon, raising hell. I said we were waiting for it to arrive.

"That afternoon, his stuff arrived and I got a call from the Sergeant. He told me the shipment was there and off to one side, out of the way. I checked out of the office and went to Receiving. The Sergeant showed me where the shipment was and I told him to go about his business and I would check the shipment out alone. Very carefully, with a bottle of paper glue, I glued the papers I had typed out the day before over every item in the shipment that had a shipping label until every item had new labels. I then called the receiving Sergeant over to the shipment and told him there had been a mistake and that this shipment was labeled to go to South Dakota. I would get a van here today, so it would be out of his way.

"The Sergeant looked at the new labels and knew what I had done. He just smiled and said this guy must be a really bad dude. I said he was. I shook his hand and told him that I was being discharged from the Air Force at five o'clock and wasn't looking back. I would be out of town before nightfall.

"I called Red Ball Van and told them I had a priority move in Receiving that had to be on the road that afternoon for South Dakota. As a personal favor, I asked that my request be carried out. The man I talked with congratulated me on my discharge and hoped my replacement continued the great work I had done for them. He then offered me a job at $70,000 a year. I turned him down because I had to get out of town. It would be months before that Lieutenant would get his household goods, thanks to his uncalled for behavior toward a lowly Sergeant.

"At six o'clock, I was on the road heading out of Roswell—never to return. I had a roll of money in my pocket from driving taxis and my Air Force pay; so I decided to take a long way home and enjoy some free time for a while. I pointed my car north, taking my time. At the next town, I checked into a motel, got some supper, and then returned to my motel room to study the road atlas.

"I headed north on US-85 into Wyoming and stopped in a town called Lusk, which is where we are now. I went into a restaurant and an older gentleman was sitting at a table looking dejected. I went over to him and asked if I might join him while I had a bite to eat. He said okay but he was not in a happy enough mood to talk. I said that he didn't look too well and maybe a stranger like me could help solve his problem. He answered that you work all year on your farm and have a few dollars in the bank and the darn property tax bill comes in the mail and your savings are almost wiped out. 'I have a 2,000-acre farm,' he said, 'and I can barely keep showing a profit. My two kids and their families work fulltime on the farm with me, and we just don't know what to do. Farming is the only thing we know and none of the farms around here are hiring help because they are in the same fix.'

"I told him that I was just discharged from the Air Force and on my way home to Michigan. I knew I was going to be in a bind because my father's farm was only 160 acres, and if I got married, the farm wouldn't make enough to support two households. At least with the size of his farm, there might be a way to make it more profitable.

"He looked up at me and said he would sure like to know how, and he would do almost anything as long as it was legal. I told him that we were both in a fix and I had a plan. 'If we teamed up, we both might come out ahead,' I said. I had been thinking about a plan for myself and my father, but his farm was just too small to make it work.

"He asked what my plan was and I told him I wasn't going to reveal it to him until I had a good appraisal of his operation. 'Give me two days to look it over while I stay at your home. If I think the plan has a chance, I will disclose what I have in mind. Otherwise, I will be on the road to return to Michigan,' I said.

"I was old school in dealing with people, and a handshake on an agreement was gospel and would be honored fully. He said, 'Do you know what you're asking me to do?'

"'To put your trust in me, an ex-Sergeant,' I answered.

"He studied me for a long time. Finally, he said, 'You drive a good bargain, mister. I'll take a chance on your honesty, there's no money at stake. My name is Tony, by the way.'

"We both paid our tab and left the restaurant together. I said I would follow him to his farm. After driving five or six miles, with a few turns to the right and left, we pulled into a driveway that led to an early-20th-century farmhouse and a nice collection of well-kept barns. I did not see any equipment. He led me into the house and introduced me to his wife, Mary. He explained to her why I was there and that he was going to show me the farm operation and fields. She looked distraught; her eyes seemed swollen and red. It was obvious that she had been crying. Mary said she would have fresh coffee ready when we got back.

"He took me on a tour of the barns and the implements stored inside. The equipment showed that he took excellent care of them and they were ready to do their jobs. A very good sign so far. We climbed into his four-wheel drive pickup and started the tour of his property. As he drove, he told me how large the fields were and what he was going to plant in them come spring. One field we were passing was mostly bare of snow, so I asked him to pull over. I wanted to examine the soil by touch. He obliged and we both got out and walked into the field. I dug a clump of dirt out with my pocketknife, squeezed it, felt it with my fingers, looked it over carefully, and then replaced it back in the divot. I did this on other fields that we passed, never making a comment on any of them. When we returned to the farmhouse, I said I wanted to look over a couple of the barns again. He followed me but did not question why or what I was doing. We then returned to the farmhouse and his wife.

"Mary had a fresh pot of coffee and cookies waiting for us when we stepped into the dining room. The coffee smelled great and, as I took a bite of a peanut butter cookie, I complimented her on how delicious the cookie tasted. She did not question her husband about what we were up to; I knew she trusted her husband in whatever he had in mind. As we chatted, he seemed to relax. I told them I was a farm kid, raised on my father's farm in Webster Township northwest of Ann Arbor. Mary asked what road the farm was on and I told her at the junction of Jennings Road and the Old Church Road. She exclaimed that she had grown up on Maple Road and backed up to that farm, which was the Grostic place. I replied that her farm must be the Kleinschmidt's. We sat in amazement as we realized our two families had been neighbors 1,200 miles to the east. If there had been any restraint between us, it had totally vanished. All our troubles were forgotten, at least for the time being. "Eventually I asked Tony to provide me with all of the expenses and receipts for the farm because I needed to review the financial structure of the operation. He replied, "No problem" and retrieved them from an old roll top desk in the sitting room. While he was getting the papers, I asked Mary how she helped on the farm. She said that one of her many jobs was to keep the books and that before their marriage she had worked for an accountant in Ann Arbor.

"Tony brought in three file folders labeled expenses, receipts, and financial statements. I remarked that there were no cigar or shoeboxes and that she knew what she was doing. She remarked that I was the first person to ever compliment her on her accounting skills and thanked me for doing so. Mary said that maybe after dinner we could all go through them together item by item. She then told Tony to get off his butt and get me settled in for my stay tonight.

"Tony and I went to my car. On the way, he asked me what my job had been with the Air Force. I told him I handled the paperwork for all in and outgoing freight for the base and processed all moving van orders for airmen being transferred to and from the base. A good friend of mine and myself drove taxicabs at night. He said that would make for a full day's work and I agreed.

"After dinner and washing the dishes, we sat around the dining room table and started examining the accounts payable and receivable files. On occasion I had a question as to the nature of an entry and Tony had a ready response every time. The receivable accounts was money received from the sale of the farm's crops. Mary had made a Xerox copy of all checks received and had them attached to the receipts from the feed and grain wholesalers. The receipts had the quantity listed as pounds or bushels and from that it was possible to calculate the product yield per acre. Mary added up all of the accounted measures and divided that figure by the total acres for the crop and that gave us the number of bushels of yield per acre. The figure she came up with per acre of corn planted was not the greatest and we discussed that at great length.

"We re-examined the acres planted for correctness, the number of bushels of corn that the mill had paid him from the receipts. Was there a possibility that the mill had short changed the payment for the graded quality listed on the receipt? The only other possibility was not enough fertilizer had been applied or the soil was worn out. I asked Tony how the soil tested for acidity or sweetness and he replied that he had no idea because his yields had always been very good so he had never had it tested. He remarked quietly that he had been a damn fool and should have known better.

"I asked him when he had last had the county Ag agent

inspect his land, and he again said never. I suggested that both of these issues be addressed immediately so plans could be made before spring planting. Mary said she would contact the county Ag agent first thing Monday morning for an appointment. I then asked Tony if his corn bin levels appeared to be lower than previous year's crops. He said not that he had noticed. I then asked Tony about crop rotation. He replied he had done some rotation but realized he should have done more. He had not been paying attention to what should have been done.

"To soften these revelations, I said that when everything appears to be going well, anyone can be negligent and what had been discovered was correctable. When times are good, we get lazy. And when there are tough times, we start looking for causes. That's what we were doing.

"I then asked Tony and Mary to list on their notepads every crop that the farmers in the area planted as supplemental crops and also for the purpose of crop rotation. I asked Mary to combine the two lists into one, deleting any duplicate entries. The combined list was short. I then asked them to list any crop they thought would be possible to grow here and I would do the same. My list was the longest, although not necessarily the best. Mary made a master list from the three lists that filled a legal pad.

"With this master list, we discussed each crop; specifically, the salability within 200 miles; possible local sales, such as farmers markets; problems that would be encountered in harvesting the crop; weather conditions that would have an adverse effect; length of growing season; and, finally, what kind of proceeds could be had from the crop. I then asked what crops could be planted that would enrich the soil if they were plowed under. This question took them both by surprise and they didn't reply. 'How about clover and timothy hay?' I suggested. They both looked in amazement. Tony asked what Ag school I had attended because I seemed to know more about crops than he did. I told them that I had never attended Ag school but I liked to solve problems.

"Tony said that my plan was a beauty and as he was thanking me, I interrupted him and said that was not my plan at all. If I told them the plan that night, though, they probably wouldn't get any sleep. Mary said I had gotten them so aroused they wouldn't get any sleep anyway, so come out with it. They were both staring at me in anticipation; so I said, 'It's simple. Raise hogs.' They both broke out in loud laughter and kept saying *hogs* over and over again.

"I just sat back and smiled, waiting for them to regain control. Mary finally said, 'But they are dirty animals.'

"'On the contrary," I argued. 'They are one of the cleanest animals around. They are like hippos and rhinoceros in that their skin is very sensitive to heat; so they soak or roll in mud to cool their body. If you keep a pen clean, pigs are content. A hog pen should have a slopping floor to a floor drain and an overhead sprinkler will flush the urine and feces away, keeping the pen clean, plus it will provide relief when it is hot.' I then explained the economics. 'Now, a cow will have one calf a year, while a hog will have from twelve to sixteen piglets. If the average of four piglets die from the sow from laying on them, you still end up with twelve pigs. They will grow big enough to market in the same amount of time as a one calf. The weight between the two animals will be about the same for the amount of feed they eat. But, hogs will eat anything you give them. The price you get for a pig compared to a cow will be about half the price of a steer. That means you have ten more pig to sell for five steer. The proceeds from marketing them will be six times more than marketing two steer. Think what that will do to your bank account in one year of full operation raising hogs. You have saved the urine and feces from the hogs in large storage tanks because its high nitrogen count makes it a wonderful fertilizer for your fields. You save on fertilizer cost as a benefit. The biggest drawback is that when the urine is spread on the fields it can be smelled ten miles away and it's not very pleasant. Your neighbors might not be too happy with you until the smell goes away.

"You might also be criticized for being a damn hog farmer; so you can expect some comments from other farmers. Your answer to them is, 'Well, I made $100,000 last year off of 2,000 acres. How well did you do?' That will usually shut them up.

"They decided to become hog farmers and I returned to Michigan. I informed my parents that I was going back to school because I still had GI Bill rights. I enrolled at Michigan State University in their School of Horticulture. I found my calling there and was asked to stay on with them as an employee while I worked on my master's degree. I got my master's degree and worked, more like played, there until I retired a few years ago and moved here. Tony and Mary's children treat me like a king. This all happened because I wanted coffee and a doughnut."

It was time for me to get on the road. I thanked him for the story, we shook hands, and I continued toward Laramie.

Chapter 12

LARAMIE'S ALTITUDE IS 7,165 FEET ABOVE SEA LEVEL. Since leaving Northport, I had traveled almost 6,600 feet in altitude. Susie's gas mileage was taking a hit because of the thin air and her get-up and go had diminished noticeably.

I phoned Ronda to tell her I was in Laramie and had just exited off I-80 and was proceeding south on Route 230, heading their way. I asked how far to their road. She told me and said Bob and she would be on the lookout for me. Whew, I hadn't gotten lost and was now close to my destination.

Ronda met me at the junction to their street and I sighed with relief as I pulled to the side of the road and greeted her with a big hug. We were both happy to see each other after twenty some years. I told her I was so glad I didn't have to make the 1,500-mile trip here with a horse and wagon.

We got back into our cars and I followed her home. Bob and I greeted each other heartily. I asked to use their restroom and Ronda said she would make a fresh pot of coffee so I could reload with liquid—and we all laughed. She said she had the spare bedroom all set for me. We sat down and reminisced about the past and started to catch up on what all of us had been doing for twenty years.

Before we turned in, she asked me what I would like to do over the next few days. I said I wanted to hear stories about when she was a Ranger and take side trips around the area where she had worked. Ronda knew every road and two-track in the area. A guided tour by a former National Park Ranger was more than any traveler could possibly expect.

The next morning, after breakfast, Ronda told a story about when she was assigned to a Ranger Office in Colorado. She had been a Ranger about two years and was still learning her trade. One day, when it was slow in the office, her supervisor suggested that she and Buddy, a coworker, replace a broken fencepost at the horse corral. The horse, Jack, had apparently backed into the fence and broken it off at ground level. The corral needed to be made secure again.

Ronda and Buddy grabbed a post-hole digger and shovels from storage and proceeded to dig out the broken post. They had dug a four-foot diameter hole around the post and it still wouldn't come out, so they kept digging. As they dug deeper, they started noticing small pieces of clay pottery along with the soil. Finally, they could remove the broken post. Curious about the pottery chards, they continued digging deeper and more carefully. Larger pieces of pottery, like plates, bowls, and cups were removed. Buddy was in the hole digging when he exclaimed he had uncovered a skull.

Ronda was dating the #2 Marshall in town, Bob Boyd, whom she later married. She called him and said he needed to come to the Park office because she had something important to show him. When Bob arrived, she took him to the corral, showed him the hole that Buddy and she had dug, and he said, "So?" She told him to look into the bottom of the hole and he spotted the exposed skull. It was very possible that Ronda and Buddy had uncovered an ancient burial ground.

Bob said he was going to pull a fast one on his boss. He used his car radio to call his boss and tell him he had a dead body and to come immediately to the Ranger Office. A few minutes later, they heard a siren wailing and Marshall #1 arrived with lights and siren blaring. Marshall #1 jumped out of his car and ran over to where Buddy, Bob, and Ronda were standing looking into the hole. Marshall #1 immediately realized he had been had.

Ronda and Buddy's supervisor called the Department of Archeology State of Colorado to send someone to examine the findings. They said they would get a team together and would have them onsite in the morning. The next morning, the archelogy team examined the findings and declared it was a Native American skeleton. Several days later, after using special scanning equipment, it was confirmed that this was, indeed, an ancient burial ground and that a lot of the corral was over the remains. The Native American Tribal Office was contacted and a new site for the corral would be found.

They nicknamed the site Jack, in honor of the horse that helped in the discovery; and Buddy and Ronda were given the nickname "The Colorado Grave Diggers," which stuck with them for some time.

Chapter 13

THAT AFTERNOON, RONDA TOOK BOB AND ME FOR A drive through some of the areas she had worked. While driving Susie, Ronda pointed out places of interest and, when we could, we got out of Susie and walked around. Many areas were still inaccessible because of the snow.

Over several days, I saw beautiful hills and mountains, and flowing streams and rivers. I even saw herds of wild buffalo, deer, elk, and mountain goats.

Ronda said she loved driving Susie and that the Suburban responded to her every command. As a U.S. Park Ranger, Ronda had always driven trucks. She said Susie had a much firmer grip of the road than any of the trucks she used to drive.

The weather was beautiful; so we did our sightseeing during the daytime and left visiting for the evenings. One evening, Bob said, "Tell him about the abandoned SUV."

Looking at me, Ronda said, "Before I start that story, I want you to know that after we were married, Bob insisted in teaching me how to shoot a pistol accurately and how to take care of it. In time, I got pretty good and he gave me a 7 mm semi-automatic for Christmas. We both still practice at least once a month. He also taught me a lot of law enforcement procedures and tips so that I would never be surprised in any situation I might encounter. He always supported me as a National Park Ranger, and made sure I was ready for any situation.

"The story Bob is referring to happened a few years ago. A fellow Ranger and I had been at a two-day meeting 100 miles from Laramie. The second day, in early afternoon, the meeting ended and we were on our return trip to Laramie. As we had plenty of time to return home, we agreed to check out some of the remote trails on our way. We radioed Laramie dispatch as to what we were going to do, and started checking out various areas that were seldom visited by anyone, including the Rangers.

"On about the fourth side trip, we came upon an abandoned SUV at the base of a small mountain. As we walked closer to it, we saw the left rear of the SUV was jacked up in the air, and the spare tire and tire iron lay alongside the vehicle on the ground. Somebody was in deep trouble, isolated in the middle of nowhere, and for how long we didn't know.

"Bob's training kicked in and I told my partner to put on gloves and not to touch a thing, and I would do the same. The doors of the SUV were unlocked. I carefully opened the passenger door, opened the glovebox, and removed the registration and insurance papers. The vehicle was registered to a couple from Northern California and the license plate matched the registration slip. We carefully searched around the SUV in a wide circle and could see no evidence of footprints.

"We returned to our truck and radioed the Sheriff's department about our discovery. We asked them to check for additional information on the people and the vehicle. We also said we were going to start a search to see if we could find anyone.

"We backtracked the way we had come in, found nothing, and then started checking two tracks off of that road, but kept coming up empty. Our radio came to life and the local sheriff informed us that there was a BOL (Be on the Lookout) for the SUV. It had been stolen and was involved in a bank robbery in California. It was last spotted in Utah three weeks earlier. The thieves were armed and considered dangerous. He told us to take all precautions for safety.

"We told him that it had a flat tire and the thieves couldn't loosen the lug nuts. We think they abandoned it and were on foot. We also told the sheriff that we had put on gloves before searching the vehicle and the only parts we had touched were the passenger door handle, the glove box release, and the ownership papers. Other than that, the vehicle was as we had found it.

"The sheriff said he would send a team out to do a forensic search and have a tow truck with air equipment come and change the tire. It would take at least an hour for his men to arrive. He asked that we return to the SUV, wait for them, and to be very careful. We agreed. I got out my duffel bag and removed my 7 mm pistol and belted it on. "My partner was surprised to see the weapon because he never carried one. I told him that my husband was an ex-Marshall and told me to never go out in the field without it.

"We returned to the SUV and checked in with our office to let them know about our delay. While we waited for the Sheriff, we both kept a watchful eye on our surroundings. Finally, a Sheriff cruiser arrived, then more cruisers, and finally a tow truck. Some deputies searched the landscape, others dusted for fingerprints. The Sheriff thanked us for not disturbing the scene and dismissed us. We called Dispatch and told them the Sheriff had taken over and that we were heading to Laramie and home.

"The nearest water to that area was about twenty-five miles away. It is likely the thieves wandered into the wilderness and died. The stolen money never turned up or any stolen vehicles reported in the area; so it is probable the thieves were lying dead in that wilderness area. For us, the case was closed as an unsolved mystery."

Chapter 14

LET ME TELL YOU THE STORY OF HOW BOB AND RONDA became lifelong friends ...

In the late 1980s, Kay and I became friends with Paul and Robin, who also lived in Northport. We would help each other with various projects, including snow blowing in the winter. Robin and Ronda were sisters.

Robin and Ronda's father and grandfather lived on the same plat of land where Paul and Robin erected a manufactured home. Living next door to her grandfather made it much easier to look after him. When the grandfather died, he willed his house to Dick, Robin's and Ronda's father,).

Dick had been a typewriter-calculator repairman for most of his life and, with the coming of computers, his business died. His income was almost zero and Social Security was what he had to live on. When Dick's home was foreclosed on, he moved into his father's home. His father had built the home to some of his strange specifications.

Dick's one passion was for animals, namely raccoons and deer. He would buy the least expensive dog food by the forty-pound bag and marshmallows for the raccoons. In the warmer months, Dick would sit on his deck and feed the animals every evening and sometimes during the day. The animals came to trust him and would take the food from his hand.

Because of our friendship with Paul and Robin, Kay and I became friends with Dick and his wild animals. Kay and I frequently went to Dick's, usually with two bags of marshmallows, and fed the raccoons by hand. Dick warned us that if two raccoons wanted food from our hand, we should always throw it because they could both bite us if we held it out to them.

It was common to see fifteen to twenty raccoons in his front yard every evening. The deer would come by almost every day, but most always in the evening. In the spring, the does would bring their fawn or fawns with them and we would watch the fawns prance and play in Dick's front yard. Many of the residents in our plat took evening walks and would stop in the road and watch the deer and raccoons feed. Dick soon became known as The Raccoon Man.

Every winter, Dick's house had a serious problem with ice dams and six-foot long icicles on the roof. He didn't know how to fix it. Dick apparently had mentioned the problem to Ronda and Bob; so one summer, when they visited Dick on their two-week vacation with their two children, Kay and I were at Dick's home when they arrived. That evening it became known that Bob and Ronda were here to try to figure out how to correct the ice dam and icicle problem. I told them I had a good idea what the problems were and, if they didn't mind, I would help them every evening after work and on the weekend. I had the skill and tools to do the job.

From that moment, our friendship flourished.

It was a grueling job. Bob and Paul worked at it by day and in the evenings I helped. The girls kept us supplied with cool drinks and snacks all the time; meanwhile the kids entertained themselves at the plat clubhouse.

I lost count, but in six or seven days of hard work, a lot of improvements were made to Dick's house; including removing and replacing old shingles and rotted boards from the rooftop, adding new water and ice shields, and insulating the attic. The ice dam and icicle issues were solved.

And that's what led to the friendship Kay and I formed with Bob and Ronda.

Chapter 15

ONE EVENING, RONDA, BOB AND I GOT TO TALKING about the many duties U.S. Park Rangers had. Ronda said almost everything imaginable was possible. She explained that within the National Parks System there are different divisions, like Forestry, Archeology, Fish and Game, Permits and Clerical, Campsite Maintenance, and Control and Preservation. With over three million square acres across the country, it was a huge task.

"When hunting and fishing seasons opened, Rangers from other divisions assisted the Fish and Game Division to be sure the laws and regulations were obeyed. And, in emergency situations, we gave whatever help was needed," she said. "This way, we got to travel to different areas and nobody got bored.

"Sometimes we took fresh food supplies to the Rangers stationed in the Fire Lookout Towers scattered throughout the National Parks. Even though we were assigned to different areas, we all worked as a team, which allowed us to get to know Rangers from the other divisions.

"Many Rangers have college degrees in specific areas. I graduated from the University of Michigan in Forestry

Management. Educational levels vary—but every Ranger is an outdoors person at heart."

"What about hikers on the trails?" I asked.

"Hiking clubs came to the parks all the time, and almost always they were well organized. Their plans for where they would hike and camp were thought out," Ronda said. "And they always registered their plans and length of stay with the appropriate Ranger Station, so we almost never had a problem with them.

"It was the average family with kids that gave us the most concern. Usually they were on vacation and the kids didn't always obey the parents and so they ended up with some sort of an emergency—and it was up to us to resolve the problem. Rescues of people with turned ankles, broken bones, and head injuries were quite common. Those that registered with us—there weren't many—were given an emergency phone number for the Ranger Station in case they needed assistance. We always had a team on alert just in case.

"Typically, it was the people that didn't register beforehand that gave us the most problems. Most didn't carry enough water to last them if they got lost; and they just went on the wilderness trails having no idea of the layout of the land or what kind of terrain they would be in.

"Most families didn't even carry a compass," Ronda continued. "Although now, with cell phones, most people rely on those—which is great, if they don't run down the battery by chit-chatting! When hiking in the wilderness, a cell phone is a great emergency tool; so the best thing is for people to turn off their phones so they will work when really needed.

"Some of our Ranger Stations had much higher rates of emergency rescues than others and a lot of man hours were used to get people out of trouble. A lot of these folks were street smart where they lived, but idiots when wandering around in the wilderness.

"Don't get me wrong," she added. "We loved helping people. And many wrote us thank-you notes for our assistance. Our goal was to provide everyone with a safe, enjoyable outing in nature's paradise."

The last story Ronda told me was about a Park Ranger who was in charge of a campground that had a number of campsites close together and a particularly persistent raccoon. "It was standard procedure to instruct all campers to store their food inside their automobiles, trailers, or motor homes and not to leave any food outside in unsecured areas. Tent campers and hikers were instructed to put their food in bags and hang the bags high up in a tree.

"Even with these instructions in place, raccoons still policed campsites for stray food, usually during the night. We would live trap the peskier raccoons and relocate them several miles away from the campground. And, to identify the animals we had trapped, we spray painted their backs. Then if the animal returned we would know by its painted back. Any re-trapped animals were transported farther away and on the other side of a river; then we usually never saw them again," Ronda explained before starting the story.

"This Ranger had trapped a particularly large raccoon. When he went to get a can of spray paint, the only color he had left was fluorescent orange. He sprayed the raccoon and relocated it several miles away from the campground.

"Three mornings later, a male camper walked into the Ranger office and said he had a couple of martinis the night before and was pleasantly happy. In the middle of the night, he woke up and had to go to the bathroom. With his flashlight on, he stepped out of his tent and was greeted by an animal with two glaring eyes and a flaming orange backside.

He wanted to know what kind of animal it was that had scared the daylights out of him.

"The Ranger said he knew then that the raccoon had found its way back to the campground. However, to the camper, the Ranger only suggested he maybe had more than a couple of martinis and it might be wise to drink them earlier in the day. Not feeling like he had gotten a straight answer from the Ranger, the camper walked away. An hour later, he returned to the office and checked out of the campsite."

That evening, I told Ronda and Bob I had changed my plans. Instead of driving to Colorado Springs and New Mexico, the next day I would head east into Nebraska on my return trip to Michigan. They said they regretted my leaving and that the time had gone so fast. I thanked them for rolling out the red carpet for me, and that after so many years, our friendship was still in high gear.

PART II

Chapter 16

I DROVE INTO LARAMIE AND GOT ONTO I-80 EAST. After more than five weeks on the road, and meeting so many people, I was pleased. The adventurer had heard about many fascinating experiences from diverse people. And when these people died, their stories would die with them.

I realized I had never asked my parents what experiences they had growing up or even as adults—and I think this is true with most families in this country. There were so many questions I would like to ask my parents, but they were both deceased so I would never get the chance.

Maybe after I returned home, I would write a book about these tales. Or was I too old to take on such a task? Although I could do many things, being an author might not be one. I didn't know the first thing about grammar, spelling, and all of the facets that make a story interesting to readers. "I'll cross that bridge when I get to it," I said to myself.

I wondered what else would develop along the way. Nebraska was a large state from east to west; I'd continue stopping at towns and maybe hear a new story. The countryside became flat and the prairie was covered with fresh snow. Sometimes corn stubble protruded in the snow-covered fields. It looked like mini steeples in a vast, white town.

As I drove, my thoughts kept returning to my father and what few things he had told me of his life. He was born in 1891, in Trevorton, Pennsylvania, which was at the western end of the hard-coal mines in the central part of the state. He had a younger sister, Viola, who died about 1918 as a result of the flu epidemic that ravaged many eastern states. Whenever my father mentioned her name, even as a little kid, I knew he missed her deeply.

He did say there wasn't a whole lot to do most of the year when he was a kid, but when the snow arrived, he and his buddies would ride bobsleds down the side of the mountain and the fast speed made the runs feel terrific. He mentioned this activity to me several times, and always after telling me of the thrill, he would pause, and then with a sad look on his face, he would add that one day he lost four of his close friends when they couldn't stop their bobsled and hit a coal train broadside. They were all killed instantly. He would close with, "I never rode a bobsled again."

In the early 1900s, the automobile became more common. Back then, most houses had front porches. If people didn't go for a buggy ride or a ride through town, they would sit on their front porch and wave at their friends as they drove by, especially on sunny Sunday afternoons.

One man who lived on the main road through town, however, hated the automobiles, with their noise and backfiring. One Sunday, he decided he was going to put a stop to it. That particular day, he took a barrel of roofing nails to the roadway and sprinkled nails all over the road. It didn't take long before almost every automobile in town was sitting with its engine turned off and its owners looking at three or four flat tires on their auto. My father, who was in earshot of the man, heard him say, "By God, now I can hear the horse hooves." If the town constable hadn't stepped in to stop the mad automobile owners, there would have been a lynching right there on the main street. The man did get his message across, and the auto owners took their Sunday trips to the other end of town.

Dad attended Bucknell University. One weekend he and a college buddy rented a canoe and went canoeing on the Susquehanna River. The canoe tipped over and they both almost drowned as neither knew how to swim. That was the last time he went canoeing.

My father graduated from Bucknell University in 1915. It was the summer of 1913 or 1914 when he and a college friend took jobs with the Atlantic City Tramway. My father was the motorman who stood in the open front of the trolley and operated the throttle and brakes. His friend was the conductor and collected fares from the passengers. My father said it was good money and no hard labor was involved, but the late-night runs would get to him as the cool, salt-air breeze off the ocean and the swaying to and fro of the trolley made it difficult to stay awake.

One night, on the final run north, near the end of the line, he fell asleep at the throttle at three-quarter speed. His friend was asleep on a bench seat inside the trolley. There were no passengers onboard. He said when the trolley slammed into the roundhouse, he fell forward and advanced the throttle to full speed and the trolley jumped the track and crashed through the back wall of the roundhouse. That accident put the entire northern run out of commission until the tracks were repaired. That was the last day he and his friend worked for the Tramway as they were chewed out and fired on the spot. My father loved telling that story to my brother and me, and we got a kick from his funny laugh that he made at the end. That Tee-Tee laugh was also noted in Bucknell University 1915 yearbook.

After his university graduation, he got a job working as a civil engineer for the New Jersey Power and Light Company. Soon he was a Chief Yeoman in the U. S. Navy, stationed in New York City. He was already a Mason and he joined the Shriner s while there.

After his service and the end of World War I, Dad was contacted by the Dean of Civil Engineering at the University of Michigan to come to Michigan to run the civil engineers on a job for the state on a highway project, which he accepted. My father was a mathematician and, to him, things were either right or wrong—and if not right, it was unacceptable. Apparently some of the contractors kept trying to slip subpar gravel on the worksite and my father would reject the efforts by the contractors every time. After the job was completed, he found himself blackballed because he wouldn't let the bad gravel be accepted. That really burned him up, that he did the job right and ended up being the fall guy.

Next he signed on with the Regina Vacuum Cleaner Company in their Detroit office as the Credit Manager for the state of Michigan and Northern Ohio. The Detroit office had about ten door-to-door salesmen when the Stock Market Crash of 1929 affected the whole country. Sales were hard to make and every workday all of the salesmen would get together and talk about how bad it was—except for one man. Each day, that one man would sell as many vacuum cleaners as the rest of the crew combined. One day, my father asked him how he was so successful while the other guys were having it so difficult. His answer was that he was good at math and he had memorized the Installment Contracts so he knew what went where and would tell the purchaser what and where to fill in the contract because he could neither read nor write. Therefore, he didn't read the newspapers and he didn't own a radio; and, therefore, didn't know if the marketplace was really bad or not. He said he had mouths to feed and, when he went to work, he worked every minute and didn't have time to listen to the jabber of the other salesmen; maybe that was why he was successful. The Regina Corporation closed all of its field offices and my father was out of a job—with a wife and my brother and me to house and feed.

My father opened up the Regina Kalamazoo Agency, bought a house, and moved us to Kalamazoo where he tried to sell vacuum cleaners. I was born in 1931 and, about that time, Dad got an ear infection and lost an eardrum. Hard times fell on the family and the bank was starting to foreclose on our home when Grandpa Bowman (no relation) saw the posted notice and stepped in and bought the mortgage from the bank. He made a land contract with my folks, only asking that my father pay the interest on the loan until he got back on his feet financially. That Good Samaritan saved my family from being put out on the street like so many others. My folks eventually paid off the land contract about 1948.

Selling vacuum cleaners, or anything for that matter (he also sold radios and small appliances), was difficult in those post-Depression years. My father would take almost anything in trade in order to make a sale. Thus, our attic had a one string violin, a small accordion, a two-person non-electric vacuum cleaner that worked the opposite of a bellows for vacuum, a 22-caliber single-shot rifle, and about 100 radios of all sizes that didn't work. My brother and I used to play hide-and-seek in the attic because the stacks of radios made for great hiding places.

During World War II, Western Michigan College had the

U.S. Navy V7 and V12 school training programs. When they heard of Dad's collection of defunct radios, they offered him $5.00 apiece for them. My father agreed—if the College would carry them out of the house and take them away. The electronics would be used in the Navy Program and the cabinets would go to the Industrial Arts Department. For the first time, I saw our attic empty.

Selling vacuum cleaners was a tough job. Dad would go house to house looking for a buyer. At one house he stopped at, the housewife was very enthusiastic about having one. For demonstrations, Dad had a special device that replaced the bag. It had a white, cotton disc inside that he could use to show the woman how efficient the vacuum cleaner was. He sprinkled some dirt particles on her rug and asked where the electric power outlet was. She replied that they didn't have electricity in their house. Dad had to clean up the mess he had made with the lady's whisk broom and dustpan. From that day on, he always checked the houses he was going to stop at to be sure they had electricity.

Dad also took in used vacuum cleaners on trade, mostly Regina's, but a few Hoover's and Eureka's as well. He would repair and rebuild old Regina vacuums as needed. I remember that when I was about eight or nine years old, he would put me on a tall stool at the side of his workbench to occupy me while he worked on a vacuum. Eventually, I started handing him parts in the order required for reassembly. From that day on, he would loosen the screws on a cleaner that was to be overhauled and have me disassemble the motor and clean all of the motor parts in white gasoline. About a year later, he taught me how to remove worn-out bearings, install new bearings, and re-assemble the entire vacuum. He always checked out my work—and I don't remember him ever telling me to redo the overhaul.

Dad also had a large electric motor with shafts extending from both ends and ten-inch diameter buffing wheels attached to the shafts. Part of re-building a used vacuum cleaner was to polish all of the parts so they looked like new. The buffing compound used to polish the aluminum was black. I would put on a skull cap, breathing mask, goggles, and a too large shop coat. After polishing the aluminum parts for four hours, I would go to the main floor, to the only wash basin in the store, to clean up and get a drink of water. The new girl employees would be frightened to death when they first saw me come up from the basement. I probably looked more like a sick raccoon or a werewolf than a boy. My parents would have to console the girls and convince them all was well.

In my younger years, Father impressed on me that if I wanted more money than my allowance, I would have to work for it. That's a code I have lived by all of my life—and to give more than what is expected. Many kids today don't live by that code. It's a shame parents let them get away with it.

Chapter 17

AS A TEENAGER, I WASTED MY MONEY ON A 1936 BUICK, a 1936 Ford, and a 10-horse-power outboard that even when new was a lemon. Finally, I decided I would walk, ride my bike, or take a bus and save up for a decent automobile.

My brother, Bob, served in World War II. When he returned home after being discharged, we became closer than we had ever been. We were almost always together doing things. Bob fancied automobiles and purchased a new 1949 Ford convertible. We would cruise town looking for girls. Sometimes we would cruise the car lots, looking for a good used car for me. It had to be 1951 when we spotted a 1950 Ford business coupe with only 16,000 miles on it. We both thought it would be a great car for me. I told Bob I was about $300 short of the sales price and couldn't buy it.

Bob drove us home and he took me to our dad, who was doing the daily bookwork. Bob started the conversation and told Dad that we had found a really good car for me but I didn't have quite enough money saved to buy it. Dad stopped doing the bookwork and asked me to tell him about the car. I told him it was only one year old and had 16,000 miles, with no dents or rust, and a V-8 engine like his 1950

Ford. Dad asked Bob if it was a good buy; my brother said it was. Dad then asked me how much more money I needed. I told him I had saved $900 and needed $300 more to make the purchase. In a very serious manner, my father told me he would loan me the money and I could set the terms of repayment. If I ever missed a payment, I was never to ask him to loan me money again. I knew he meant what he said.

I was working my way through college and my parents paid the $70-per-semester tuition. I would have so much money left over each week from my earnings; and I told him I could pay so much a week. Dad said okay and pulled out a blank slip of paper and wrote I O U at the top and below the figure of $300. He had me sign it, then he wrote a check for $300. I never missed a payment; in fact; I paid him off about six weeks early. I never asked him for another loan, but I knew he would help me if the need should ever arise.

Chapter 18

DAD GREW UP IN THE MOUNTAINS OF PENNSYLVANIA; so weeding flowerbeds was not anything he had ever been exposed to. He didn't know a weed from a flower; however, he did know a bush when he saw one. One Sunday, my mother declared that after church the whole family was going to help her weed her numerous flowerbeds. She assigned each of us an area and the four of us dug into the task. Dad, in his wisdom, didn't like weeding the least bit, and removed every single sprig from his area. When my mother came to inspect all of our areas, she exploded at my father for pulling out all of the flowers along with the weeds. He explained that he didn't know a weed from a flower and they all looked alike to him. My mother never asked him to weed again—and he was pleased at that decision. I remember the smile on his face as he carried the pulled weeds and flowers to the back forty of the property.

Sometime in the early 1950s, my parents gave me a terrier mix dog for my birthday present. Cosmo was a fearless little guy and would stand his ground to any dog, regardless of its size. Cosmo and Dad took to each other and he was always at Dad's side. Cosmo loved to ride with dad when he made deliveries or went to the drive-in bank. The bank tellers all knew Cosmo and give him a bone every time they stopped at the drive-in.

My mother's attitude and personality changed toward everyone, including my dad. Their relationship became all business with no pleasure. When Kay and I were married in 1959, I left Cosmo with Dad as that was the only pleasure Dad had at home. I never told Dad, however, I think he knew why I left Cosmo with him.

I became the black sheep in the family. In 1961, I left the business and struck out on my own, hardly ever talking with them except on the streets downtown. What had once been a close-knit family was forever marred by greed and possessiveness.

I keep a picture of my father on my computer desk and wish things had worked out differently. He lived to be almost eighty-four before he passed away. Maybe because of the loss of my family ties, I take great pleasure in helping other people—even total strangers who are struggling with a problem and don't know the answer and need help.

Chapter 19

THERE WAS FRESH, WET SNOW ON THE HIGHWAY AS I continued driving eastward on I-80. It was still daylight and I didn't feel like calling it a day yet. Also I had no idea what town or city I was near.

While I was reminiscing about Dad, I lost track of my location. At the next exit I would gas up Susie and locate the town on my map. Before leaving Laramie, I had thought David City looked interesting. It was a few miles off I-80, but I wasn't concerned about that. At mile marker 373, I pulled off the interstate and into a gas station in a small town. I gassed up and bought a deli sandwich. It wouldn't be far and I would head north on Highway 15 toward David City. On the way, it started snowing; the wet kind that makes the roads slick.

When I turned onto Highway 15, I started getting that funny feeling. I was driving much slower, the snow was coming down harder, and night had arrived. There was no sense taking any chances, I thought, when suddenly, I heard a bang. It felt like metal hitting metal, and there was a sound like something was caught in the undercarriage and being dragged on the road. I pulled off to the side of the highway, grabbed my flashlight, and got out to see what was making the noise. On my hands and knees in the wet snow, I peered underneath and saw a strip of metal dangling from the lower suspension and liquid splashing out. I stood up and opened the hood. Somehow one end of the metal strip had got behind the shielding and had sliced the lower radiator hose. Anti-freeze-coolant was draining from the engine. The lower hose had a long slit in it and there was no way duct tape would ever stick to the hose because of the slimy anti-freeze. I removed the metal strip, got back into Susie, and considered my options—which weren't many.

There was no way to repair the leak on the side of the road. I turned off the engine as the temperature gauge was reading hot and put on the emergency flashers. I would let the engine cool down and just sit for a while. The car thermometer read 24 degrees, and the wind had picked up. It would be a long, cold night if I just stayed there. I figured it was closer for me to continue toward David City, where a replacement hose could be installed, rather than return to the small town where I had gassed up and no possibility of getting a new radiator hose.

The cold wind was cooling off the engine; after about thirty minutes I started up Susie and continued north. I figured I could go two miles before the engine would get too hot and I'd then pull over and wait another thirty30 minutes or so. No house lights along the road, but maybe I would get lucky and see some along the way. Three or four times I did this routine. Just before I stopped the last time, I thought I saw a glimmer, but then it vanished. Maybe it was only a reflection from my headlights. My thoughts returned to despair.

On the next two-mile segment, I saw a light in the distance and I slapped the steering wheel in joy. Another thirty minutes and I headed down a road toward the light and came on some barns and an old farmhouse with light shining out the windows. I pulled into the yard, parked Susie near the barn closest to the house, got out, and started walking toward the doorway to the house when the yard lights came on. That funny feeling came over me again as I got closer to the house. Suddenly, the door opened and a lady yelled at me to get in out of the wind and snow. She is an angel, I thought as I stepped into her kitchen.

She asked me what I was doing out in this mess and I told her of my problem. I asked if I could use her phone to call a tow truck to come and get me. She replied that I was out of luck until Monday. It was Friday night. I asked her why so long to get a tow. She replied that Max was the only guy in David City who had a tow truck, and every Friday night he would go on a weekend bender. He wouldn't be sober enough to drive until Monday morning. I suggested that if the roads were passable in the morning, she could drive me into town and I would purchase a new radiator hose. She replied the TV weatherman had just reported that this storm was going to last until tomorrow morning, and about eight to ten inches was expected. "Go get your duds from your car. You're spending the weekend here," she said.

At that point, the funny feeling vanished.

Chapter 20

WHEN I RETURNED WITH MY DUDS, SHE HAD PUT ON a fresh pot of coffee, and showed me to my sleeping quarters on the second floor. The layout and floor plan of the house was almost exactly like my grandparents' farmhouse in Ann Arbor. My grandparents' house had been purchased through a Sears Roebuck catalog in about 1903. This farmhouse had to be of the same vintage. When I told her this, she was amazed. To her, it was just home. "Now I can put some history with this dwelling, and could brag that my house came from Sears," she said.

She asked me how I liked my coffee. I said, "Black." She motioned me into the dining room and to take any chair. Soon she returned with a large mug of freshly brewed coffee. I could smell the aroma of it.

I introduced myself and she said her name was Connie McGregor. She had lost her husband three years earlier in a farming accident. Her three children had all graduated from the University of Nebraska and had gotten married. They now lived in other parts of the country; none of which were close to David City. I asked Connie if she ran the farm by herself. She explained that she managed it and her two brothers-in-law did the actual farming for her on a lease agreement.

Each of the three brothers had inherited roughly 5,000 acres from their parents, Dennis and Eileen McGregor. Last year, with the dry climate, the crop yield per acre had fallen off and after the property taxes were paid there wasn't much of a nest egg to fall back on. Another bad crop and a year like last year would spell real trouble. She said she was going to hang on as long as she could and hope for the best.

I mentioned that McGregor was a Scottish name. "Were the three boys born in Scotland?" I inquired.

She replied, "The boys' parents, Dennis and Eileen, were married in Scotland and had been sponsored by Jim, an American friend Dennis made while in the military. I don't know all of the particulars, except Jim was employed by his father in the farm implement business in Lincoln, Nebraska. Jim had a farmer client that was thinking about selling his 5,000-acre farm near David City. Jim told Dennis in a letter that it was a choice piece of land, with implements that were in great shape.

"Dennis's parents had both died and their farm had been left to Dennis, their only son. Dennis had commented to Jim that he was tired of trying to farm rocks in Scotland. If Dennis could raise the necessary capital, Jim said he would negotiate a deal for the Nebraska farm.

"Dennis met with his two uncles to sell them his farm. True to form, the uncles were thrifty Scots and didn't want to pay the price Dennis wanted. Dennis had to impress on them that his farm was the best in the area and was certainly better than the ones they owned. The selling price and offered price became much closer but neither party would give in. Dennis then said he would include all of the livestock, tools, equipment, and the farmhouse for so many more dollars, and they could make a deal. The farmhouse had never been mentioned in any of the negotiations; so including the farmhouse was a total surprise to the uncles because they had assumed the farmhouse was already included. Dennis had put one over on the uncles, and they knew it.

"Dennis told his uncles they had three days to make a decision and if they didn't come to terms, the entire property would go on the market. The uncles objected but Dennis held his position and wouldn't budge. Three days later, the uncles agreed to buy the entire property by a certain date.

"Dennis and Eileen applied for immigration to the USA. Dennis wrote Jim to start negotiations on the Nebraska property and that he had so many American dollars to work with. The immigration application was accepted and tickets were purchased for a ship going to New York City.

"Jim and his wife met Dennis and Eileen in New York City, and the four of them headed to Nebraska in Jim's auto; visiting sites and farms along the way. They spent some time around Lancaster County farmland and visited a number of Amish farms and took note of their way of life. The Indiana countryside also impressed Dennis and Eileen—all of the crops were so much better than what they had tried to grow in Scotland. Crop yield had to be tremendous and the industrial might of this nation was unbelievable. They totally believed that immigrating to the United States was the best thing they could ever have done.

"Dennis thought of his uncles and felt sorry for the land conditions they had to work with. Dennis asked Jim if the land he had bought in Nebraska was the same as what they had seen so far. Jim answered, 'It is even better.'

"They traveled across Illinois, eastern Iowa, and into Nebraska; finally reaching Lincoln. Dennis and Eileen could hardly control themselves in wanting to see their new farm.

Jim told them they would leave early tomorrow to drive to David City and they could see the farm for themselves.

"They were so excited, they could hardly contain themselves. Jim's home was on the outskirts of Lincoln, and the fields of corn could be seen beyond his backyard. Dennis kept going outside and looking at the standing corn. Finally he asked Jim to join him to go stand in that tall cornfield. Dennis told Jim that if his new farm was anything like this piece of land, he would be forever in his debt.

"The next day they were all on their way to David City. Dennis and Eileen gazed out the car windows the entire drive; their excitement growing with each passing mile. Without any warning, Jim slowed the car and pulled into a farmyard that had a large, two-story farmhouse, three large barns, and several other building for various uses. Jim exclaimed, 'Here's your new digs, old buddy!'

"Dennis and Eileen jumped out of the car. Dennis ran to the standing corn, then to each of the barns and outbuildings. Eileen grabbed Jim's wife's hand and said, 'We have to see the house!' Jim unlocked the house and the two women disappeared inside. He could hear them chattering and exclaiming to each other as they checked out every room; especially the kitchen.

"The house had been purchased furnished and ready to move in. They had a deed without a mortgage—it was all theirs. Eileen took Jim's wife's hand, and whispered, 'I haven't told Dennis yet, but I'm pregnant.' They hugged each other in joy.

"When the guys entered the house, Eileen walked over to Dennis, put her hands on his shoulders, and said, 'I'm pregnant.' When Dennis recovered from the news, he put his arms around her, picked her up, and started dancing a jig around the room while Jim and his wife clapped their hands in joy."

Chapter 21

CONNIE CONTINUED HER STORY. "DENNIS AND EILEEN had three children. All were boys in the truest sense. The firstborn was George; he married Theresa Marie. The second son, Lenny, married me. The third son was Phil; he married Julie.

"Dennis and Eileen had saved enough money to send all three sons to the University of Nebraska. Two of them graduated in their own field of study with Agriculture as their major. All of us three girls met our future husbands at the university and were married after graduation. George and Theresa Marie moved in with my in-laws. During the years when Lenny and Phil were in school, Dennis and Eileen purchased two farms with about 5,000 acres each. After Lenny and I were married, we moved into the second farm and were assigned to manage it and the livestock. The same happened to Phil and Julie.

"The farms we lived in were later deeded to each son and his spouse. The only condition was that each family would help the other two brothers. Dennis and Eileen became grandparents; then Eileen became ill and within six months, she passed away from cancer. Dennis could never cope with the loss of his wife, and he finally just gave up and died.

They had a wonderful life together; it's a shame it had to end as it did.

"Our three families all had multiple children, and we sent all of them to the University of Nebraska and, like us, they all married after graduation. This time though, the children and their spouses took jobs in other parts of the country, with none within 100 miles of here. In a way, this was a blessing because the three families became more attached to each other. Each Sunday after church we would rotate homes for a Sunday afternoon gathering.

"When Lenny was killed in the farming accident, his brothers and their wives would always come here to try to cheer me up. That helped me a lot, but I still feel empty inside and miss Lenny every day. I ask myself why the accident had to occur. Lenny was always so very careful around machinery and always turned off the equipment before he would get off. This one time, he didn't and he was having a conversation with George when he backed into the blades and had an artery severed. George tried to render first aid but Lenny bled to death in his arms. I can tell George carries that accident with him all the time."

To break the sadness in Connie, I told her she was a mighty fine, good-looking, trim grandmother and didn't show her age. She responded, "Thank you. But wait until you see my two sisters-in-law on Sunday afternoon at our weekly gathering."

About that time, a chime clock struck eleven o'clock. We agreed to go to bed as chores started at six. I told her I would milk the cow so she could stay out of the cold. Connie looked at me with a funny face and asked how I knew how to milk a cow. I told her I used to milk when I was a boy.

We both turned in for the night.

Chapter 22

THE NEXT MORNING, I AWOKE TO A NOISE DOWNstairs. My watch said 5:45. Time to put on my travel clothes and go milk a cow. I met Connie in the kitchen and told her I needed a couple of pails. I was going to milk her cow. She asked me when I had last milked a cow. I thought for a moment, then answered. "About seventy years—but some things you just don't forget." She handed me a metal pail. I said, "I need two."

"One should be enough," she replied. "Bessie is old and doesn't give that much milk anymore."

"Give me another one, just in case," I insisted. She did.

Off to the barn I went, with two milk pails. The old barn had sliding doors throughout. After going through three sliders, I entered the milking parlor where Bessie was lying down in a stanchion. I addressed Bessie with a cheery, "Good morning, Bessie!" and she rose to her feet. "You need hay and oats to start the day off. I'll fill your water bucket before I start milking."

She looked at me with two sad eyes and watched me get her feed. She dug right into the hay while I went to the grain bin and got a coffee can of oats and filled her water container. She had eaten most of the hay, so I held a handful of oats in front of her. Bessie gently licked the oats and I gave her more handfuls until all the oats were gone.

I grabbed the two milk pails and entered the parlor, looking for the milking stool. I saw a three-legged stool off to one side. That stool wouldn't do for me. I wanted the kind that my grandfather had used and taught me how to use. I gave Bessie a good rub on her shoulder and told her I would be back in a few minutes. Bessie looked at me in wonderment and then started eating the rest of the hay.

I went into the shop area of the barn and found an eleven-inch-square board and an old, broken, shovel handle. I cut a section about ten inches long from a straight part of the handle and found a three-inch wood screw. I drilled a pilot hole through the center of the board that was big enough for the screw to go through and stop at the head. I then drilled a smaller hole into the end of the round shaft and screwed the two pieces together.

I found a rasp and rounded the edges and corners of the board and squatted down on the board with the single rod on the floor. The height seemed about right for milking. With my new one-legged milk stool, I returned to Bessie. Bessie had emptied her water container and so I refilled it for her. She emptied it again. I repeated this several times until she finally had all she wanted.

I found a clean cloth and cleaned her teats, then grabbed a pail and my new stool. I showed Bessie the stool, which she studied. Then I got into position to milk her. I started humming a tune called "The Thing" that Phil Harris had recorded in the early 1950s and commenced milking her. Bessie was letting a lot of milk come; obviously content having a stranger milk her. I stroked her to the rhythm of the song. Before I knew it, the pail was three-quarters full and I was only half done and had two more teats to do. I started doing the last two teats and the pail was soon half full when Connie walked into the parlor and asked if I was having a hard time of it. I said no and nodded to the pail off to the side that was three-quarters full. I kept on stroking.

Connie looked into the pail, then to the three-legged stool off to the side, and then back at me. Eying the one-legged stool, she asked, "Where did you find that stool?" I told her I made it from scraps I found in the shop. If a cow kicks you while milking, you won't land as hard because you fall off faster.

I told Connie she could take the first pail to the house and I would be along directly after I finished. I also asked her if she wanted Bessie left in her stall or let outside in the barnyard. Connie told me to open the barn door and unlock the stanchion. If Bessie wanted outside, she would go out on her own. When Bessie was finished, I removed the pail. It, too, was three-quarters full. I placed it out of the way and opened up the door. Bessie wanted outside. I gave her a gentle rub behind her ears and she walked into the barnyard.

I cleaned the parlor with a shovel and broom, closed the barn door, and headed for the house with the second pail of milk. In the kitchen, Connie looked into the second pail and exclaimed, "Bessie hasn't given that much milk in years! What did you do to cause the increase in production?"

"Well," I said. "Bessie and I got acquainted and I fed her all she wanted. I hummed a tune while I milked her, and we just took our time."

Connie looked confused. "You only took fifteen to twenty minutes longer than what it takes me—and you got twice as much milk." She shook her head, thinking. As we ate, she would look at me with a strange look on her face, then return to studying her food. Suddenly she asked, "Just who are you anyway?"

Chapter 23

CONNIE'S QUESTION CAUGHT ME OFF GUARD. IT WAS two-sided. One side was my name, where I reside, what I did for a living, what I enjoyed doing for recreation, etc. These could be easily answered. The other side of the question was much more complex because it involved other aspects of my life. After some hesitation, I said it would take me a while to give her a definitive answer.

She replied, "That was a terrible thing to ask. I'm sorry."

"No. You have every right to know who is living in your home, eating your food, and exchanging conversation," I replied. After some time and without too much rambling, I shared my history with Connie.

"As a young lad, most of my time was spent alone, with no friends to play with. Both of my parents worked all day and my older brother was usually off doing something with friends his age. Looking back, I would say I was a very lonely boy and, other than the radio, there was no sound in the house. My fellow students in grade school were from other parts of the city or county, and the closest schoolmate lived a mile away so I just stayed home and did my assigned chores, listened to the radio, and sometimes did homework.

My parents were always tired from their day's work and never asked if they could help me. And I was usually tired also, so just went to bed.

"In high school, I liked sports, especially football and basketball. This gave me interaction with other students. I earned a varsity letter my freshman year for being on the defensive line of our football team. I was big for my age and none of the other players messed with me or tried to bully me. At long last, I felt that my teammates respected me and my abilities.

"My sophomore year of football was great until my left knee was severally injured in the second game of the season. After twenty days on crutches, my doctor told me that if I ever re-injured that knee I would need surgery to put it back together. I was devastated. After that, I did play clarinet in the high school band and orchestra.

"Each day after school I worked in my parents' store for spending money. I never had a close friend or buddy to associate with. My father, except on rare occasions, would not let me use the family auto; so dating girls in my class just didn't happen. The girls I had an interest in were from affluent families and riding a bus on a date would be beneath them. My brother, after serving in World War II, would spend weekend daytimes with me, but at night he was busy chasing girls or budding up with his friends.

"I worked a lot and paid my own way through four years of college; had a bad experience with junker automobiles; and did, at long last, have a girlfriend. She mentioned that she wanted to get married, so I broke off the relationship because I couldn't afford to support a family and I didn't want to live with my parents when married. The one pleasure I did have was meeting and helping people in my parents' business and other employments I've had over the years. My mechanical skills developed over the years and my willingness to help people resolve their problems was commonplace.

"I did meet a lovely lady, Kay, and we married in 1959. We built a new home on a hillside with a beautiful view. We started by digging the basement ourselves, using a wheelbarrow and shovels. When it was completed, it would have four levels. When we moved in, there were only two levels with a leaky, flat roof. Money was always a problem; however, after five years, we had a completed home. Problems developed between our two families and having children never came about.

"After having four different jobs, all low-pay, we settled in Northport, in Northern Michigan, and I went to work in a hardware store, working part-time during the winter months. In the spring, the owner asked me to work fulltime, which I gratefully accepted. The pay was reasonable and it was the last job I held. Everybody who goes to a hardware store has a problem and I really liked helping people out in any way I could. I try to recognize potential problems before they happen and come up with what I think is the best solution.

"Some of my solutions are from trial and error—if you do something over a few times, you don't forget. Many friends were made in the thirty-two years I worked at the hardware store, and for the first time in my life, I felt like I belonged. I have made new friends in open bowling and in league play, and I play in the Northport Community Band. Kay passed away in 2015, and now I am lonely again, which is why, I guess, I'm taking this trip—to get people back into my life again. People's stories and experiences energize me. It is a joy listening to them tell them.

"Connie," I said, "that's the gist of my life. I enjoy being a Good Samaritan to everyone I meet; so I guess that's who I am."

All was quiet between us for a bit.

I finally broke the silence. "I haven't fed the hogs yet."

"Wow, I need a cup of coffee after all of this!" Connie finally said. "You feed the hogs. I already fed the chickens. I'll get a fresh brew of coffee going."

We both stood up from the table and she came over to me and gave me a big hug. As I carried the surplus milk to the hog pen, I said to myself, "What's happening between us? I have never told anyone about my life before—and in less than twenty-four hours I have let it all out to Connie, my new friend."

Chapter 24

AS I RETURNED FROM THE HOG PEN, IT QUIT SNOWing. It felt like the wind had changed to the southwest and the temperature was rising. I shared this news with Connie when I entered the kitchen and removed my boots.

I got my Auto Club card from my wallet and dialed the number for roadside assistance. After a few selections, I had a live person on the line. I explained my dilemma. Because I wasn't in Michigan, the woman put me on hold while she contacted the Nebraska Auto Club. About eight minutes later she came back on the line and told me a tow truck would arrive at my location in about an hour. It would transport Susie to the Chevrolet Garage in David City. They would try to have my car repaired by noon today. Because I had hit an object in the road, my Comprehensive Coverage would apply. I would need to pay the $50 deductible and should have my membership card ready for the tow truck driver. My transportation problem was going to be resolved in record time, even though it was a Saturday.

Twenty minutes later the tow truck pulled into Connie's yard and a young man backed his truck up to Susie. Connie went outside with me. "Good morning, Mrs. McGregor," he said.

Connie greeted the young man and jokingly said, "Hi, Bill. What took you so long getting here?"

As Bill winched Susie onto his truck, Connie explained to me that Bill was a close friend of her son's and they still kept in touch, even though they lived hundreds of miles apart.

Connie asked Bill if he had an empty cup or mug as she would refill it for him. He stopped what he was doing and retrieved a big mug from the cab and handed it to Connie. "You make the best coffee," he said. "Better than what I can get in town."

After Bill had Susie securely on his truck, I signed the work order and gave him a $50 check. As he drove away, he said to Connie, "You really look great this fine morning. I'll bring my wife and little girl out to see you soon."

I didn't know it then, but Connie must have heard me tell Bill I was going to be eighty-five the next day and having Susie repaired so quickly was his birthday present to me.

Connie and I returned to the house.

She set two big mugs of fresh coffee on the dining room table. In the center of the table was a plate of homemade cookies. "Dig into the cookies before they go stale," she said as I sat down.

I took a cookie and told her I was a cookie monster and never turned down homemade cookies.

"Me, too," she said and took a bite.

"You've filled me in on yourself," I said, "but you haven't said much about your in-laws. How do they fit into your life?"

"They're the best friends I have. We all support each other in whatever we do. The three brothers—George, Lenny, and Phil—were all different. George, the firstborn, is a character and takes a lot of getting used to, at least for me. He can be gruff and obnoxious at times, and he commands attention from everyone when in a gathering. He's kindhearted under all that gruffness, and people outside the family usually give him a wide berth. George goes full blast in whatever he's doing, and quite often messes up and has to do things over.

"Farming is all he thinks about, every day. His parents were from Scotland and they spoke with a Highland dialect and George learned that dialect from them. That's the way he talks. He can speak English, but he prefers not to. It's difficult to understand him when he gets wound up, and us girls have to keep asking him to slow down and speak clearly. Even Theresa Marie sometimes has a hard time understanding him—and she really lets him have it! That makes George mad with her because by the time she can understand him he's lost his train of thought and gets upset. She just calmly tells him to talk like an American and then she wouldn't interrupt him. Theresa Marie has told Julie and me that she plays that game with him mostly in fun—and George has never caught on.

"All three of us girls, and Lenny and Phil, graduated from the University of Nebraska with different majors; so we have expertise in five areas. George went to the university one year and nearly flunked out because they couldn't understand his speech and he wrote like he talked. When George dropped out, he declared that book learning didn't teach him how to farm. Theresa Marie's major was music; she can play almost any instrument, and she made sure their children could perform music with any instrument of their choosing. All of their kids could play an instrument by the time they were five years old. Even though they could play any instrument, she taught all of them how to play the mouth organ. George's instrument was drums and any percussion piece that made a noise. Drums are his instrument of choice but he can also play the euphonium and tuba. They all fit his personality perfectly.

"Phil and Julie met at the university and were married right after graduation. Dennis and Eileen turned over a 5,000-acre farm with a house for them to manage. Phil had a dual major in Agriculture and Electronic Engineering. He graduated in the top ten percent of his class. He is one smart guy and becomes an expert on any subject he chooses to learn about. He's an encyclopedia on all farming practices and new technology that comes out. He's in regular contact with the State Department of Agriculture and they often call him for information they need. Julie majored in Nursing and is an RN. Sometimes she helps out at the David City Hospital. She learned to play the flute and oboe and played in ensemble groups while at the University. Phil plays the trombone mainly, and can also play the French horn, which is a difficult instrument to play. Phil is a quiet fellow, but when he plays the trombone he really comes to life and lives it up with lots of movement. If you want to get information on something, ask Phil. If medical advice is needed, I call Julie.

"My Lenny was a mixture of George and Phil. He was especially good with anything mechanical, especially farm implements. Unlike George, he was soft spoken and would give his full attention to me when we talked. He would always take time to help me with my chores, in the house and farm. He would talk to the animals or hum a tune, like you said you did to Bessie.

"You remind me of Lenny, a lot Lenny's major was Agriculture and a minor in Business Studies. He played the clarinet in ensembles, like Julie. We were married right after graduation and Dennis and Eileen set us up with this farm. Lenny died in the field on this farm.

"The scope of knowledge and skills each of us has makes for a perfect team; not matched by any farm from here to Lincoln.

"While Dennis and Eileen were alive, the entire family got together every Sunday afternoon for dinner and playtime for all of our kids. Eileen died first, and I think Dennis died with a broken heart one year later. All of their grandchildren are married and have children of their own. Theresa Marie, Julie, and I are all grandmothers now, but the kids have moved to other parts of the country and hardly ever get home. In farming, you just can't pack a bag and leave the farm. We are all tied down and can't visit our kin like we did with Dennis and Eileen.

"I think not having a family around and then losing your spouse really makes it hard. Even the short time you've been here has made me feel much better emotionally. I thank you for that." As Connie made that last statement, her hands started to shake. She gripped them together to stop the shaking.

This lady needed help 24/7, I thought. That weird feeling I had on the road brought me to help Connie gain closure on the passing of Lenny. I would have to return home to pay my taxes and to catch up on prepaying other obligations—somehow I would do that and still give Connie the help she badly needed.

It was about 11:30 and the phone rang. My car was fixed and would be delivered shortly.

Changing the subject, I asked Connie to call Theresa Marie and Julie to have them bring their instruments over for a Sunday afternoon jam session. Her eyes lit up and she said she was going to call them right away and for me to excuse her while she did so.

Both sisters-in-law, upon answering Connie's call, wanted to know if something was the matter. They both said they'd be over immediately. Connie laughed into the phone and told them that she was calling for a jam session on Sunday afternoon. They said there wasn't a clarinet player. Connie told them she had that covered. They didn't ask how, and Connie didn't tell them that I was here.

Connie said it was lunchtime and she had some hard-boiled eggs and would make egg salad sandwiches. "Great! I said. "And as long as the sun is shining and the snow is melting, we should take a walk around the farm after lunch."

She said it was a marvelous idea. She had been cooped up all winter, and a walk in the sunshine would be good for the soul. After lunch, we put on our boots and had an enjoyable walk around the farm. We chatted about nothing in particular.

Returning to the farmhouse, Connie got her mail and went inside while I brushed the snow off Susie. When I returned to the house, I asked Connie if there were any barn dances or a movie we could attend that evening. She said she would have to check the newspaper. Not since Lenny had died had she checked out the entertainment section.

Connie seemed thrilled with the idea of getting out of the house for an evening of fun. She found a dance hall; so we decided to go there after dinner. By ten-thirty we were both bushed and our clothes were sweaty from dancing almost every dance in the warm dance hall. We called it a night and returned to Connie's home. We were both exhausted from such a wonderful evening.

Chapter 25

IT WAS ABOUT A QUARTER TO FIVE WHEN GEORGE announced they had to get home and do chores. We were all in Connie's dining room. Phil asked me when I was going to leave for Michigan. I said I wanted to do some maintenance on the machinery for Connie before I left. Phil said that everything should be ready to go as George had cleaned them up after last year's harvest. I replied that everything was coated with dirt and pressure hoses were leaking fluid and stuff like that. Phil told Theresa Marie to sit tight while he checked on what I had said.

At a brisk walk Phil, George, and I walked to the equipment barn. Phil walked in first, turned on the lights, and said, "What the hell?!" He walked directly to the big tractor and looked inside. It was a dirty mess. He removed two empty whiskey bottles, raised the engine cowl, and looked inside to another dirty mess of oil oozing from the valve covers. He went to a workbench, grabbed a clean rag, and went back to the tractor and pulled out the oil dipstick. I was by his side and George was standing in front of the tractor watching Phil. Phil stared at the dipstick in amazement and yelled at George, "When in hell did you change the oil in the tractor last?" George just shrugged his shoulders. "Answer me, dammit!" yelled Phil. George very quietly said he didn't remember.

I touched Phil with a hand and pointed to the end of the dipstick. "That is pure carbon-solid sludge stringing from the end. My guess is it has to be at least three-eighths of an inch thick in the bottom of the oil pan. If that is true, the oil hasn't been changed since before Lenny died. The oil filter is probably plugged solid too."

Phil then inspected each of the vehicle cabs, removing empty whiskey bottles and one bottle that was almost empty. Phil whirled toward George and yelled, "You haven't done anything but run the equipment and maybe add oil if it was low. Probably every machine in here is in the same, if not worse, condition. If you needed help to do the maintenance, all you had to do was ask me. Now, we have a disaster on our hands. I hope we can salvage what's left." As he headed toward the farmhouse, he kept muttering, "Damn. Damn. Damn."

I stopped at Susie, grabbed my recorder, and followed Phil, with George tagging along behind us with his head bowed down. When we were all in the dining room, I turned on my recorder and put it on the table. Phil shoved George into a chair and blew his gasket. He ripped George up one side and down the other, desperately trying not to use profane language. The girls stood in amazement, as never had they heard Phil tear into anybody like he was doing to George. George just sat there in a stupor, not saying a word.

Julie interrupted Phil and sternly asked what was going on. Phil flopped down into a chair and held his head between his hands for the longest time, not saying a word. Julie went to Phil and put her hand on his shoulder and squeezed firmly. That brought Phil back to life and he calmly told us that because of lack of maintenance and long hours of use, a half million dollars of Connie's equipment was probably junk, unless by some miracle it could be repaired.

All three girls slumped into chairs and stared from George to Phil. The room was dead quiet for the longest time.

I took hold of George's chair and turned it so it faced parallel to the table. Then I took an empty chair and placed it in front and facing George. I asked Julie if she had a medical kit with her. She said yes, it was in the trunk of their car. I told Phil to get the medical kit and bring it inside to Julie. I told Julie to check George's vitals and to leave the cuff on him. When Phil returned, she sat down in front of George and started to take his vitals. I pulled up a chair and sat down beside her.

I looked at Julie and told her to quietly monitor George as I questioned him. If his vitals were okay, she should give a thumbs up; and if not so good, give a thumbs down. She knew I wanted complete silence during my quizzing. She put a finger to her lips and looked at the others in the room.

I told George to look me straight in the eye and that I was going to ask him questions and to nod yes or no if he didn't want to speak. I then placed Julie's free hand on George's free hand and whispered for her to grip his hand for responses. "George," I said, "I'm going to ask you some questions and I want truthful answers. Julie and I will know if you are lying or avoiding the truth."

He nodded approval.

"You really loved your dad and mother?"

He nodded yes.

"You really miss your dad, don't you?"

He nodded yes.

"You and your dad were extremely close?"

He nodded yes.

"You would do almost anything for your dad. You even talk and walk like him too."

He nodded yes.

"Your whole family used to sit on the front porch each evening and watch the breeze blow through the cornstalks."

He nodded yes.

"Your dad always had a pint of his ale, and when you were about fourteen years old he gave you a little from his glass?"

He nodded yes.

"Did it taste great to you?"

He nodded yes.

"As you grew older, he would bring you some ale in your own glass?"

Yes.

"When you were seventeen or eighteen, he would give you a full pint each evening and some in the morning, and at the noon meal and afternoon break—whenever he would have his drink?"

Yes, again.

All of us in the room now knew the root of George's problem. George was fast becoming alcohol dependent. No one had been aware of the problem—and neither had George.

"After graduating from high school, your parents wanted you to have a college education and they enrolled you in the University of Nebraska."

Yes.

"You didn't learn well and sloughed off most of the time, partying with those who could buy beer. You finished your first year with Cs and Ds."

Yes.

"The best thing that happened to you was meeting and dating Theresa Marie."

George smiled a little at that statement, then his expression went blank again.

"During summer break, you couldn't see her; so you wrote letters to her every week and she answered them."

Yes.

"When fall term started, you would drive to Lincoln every Sunday to see her, and soon you asked her to marry you. She didn't turn you down, but said she would not marry until after she had graduated from the university. You started having seconds of the ale and your dad didn't seem to mind; in fact, he would have seconds also."

Yes.

"Sometime in her third or fourth year of college, you brought Theresa Marie home to meet your mom, dad, and Phil. She had already met Lenny because he was going to Nebraska also."

Yes.

"In her senior year, you again asked her to marry you. She accepted and you were married after graduation."

Yes.

"Dennis and Eileen welcomed Theresa Marie with open arms and made an apartment in their big house for you two to live in."

Yes.

"Your family became five members, and the farm was great, and your mom spoiled your kids with delight. Your dad purchased this farm just before Lenny and Connie were married and fixed it up for them to live in and raise a family. No problem there, as your family was happy where they were. Two years later, Phil and Julie were married after they graduated, and Dennis purchased another farm for them to live in."

Yes.

"A few years later, your mom got cancer, and after six months of suffering, she passed, leaving Dad a widower. A year later, he passed away. Everyone thought he died from heartache from the loss of his wife. But really, it was from kidney failure due to drinking alcohol for so many years."

George's head snapped up. He had never heard about his dad's kidney failure.

"In his will, he left each of you the farms where all of you live now."

Yes.

"You and your two brothers made a great team. Each of you with different abilities that made your three farms the most successful in the county. Everything seemed perfect, except your dad's ale supply was getting low; so as a substitute, you switched to drinking Scotch whiskey. You had bottles stashed in all of the barns and farm equipment, and in your truck—so a bottle was always available."

George started to shake his head no.

I barked at him not to lie.

He then nodded yes.

Julie started wiggling her thumb up and then down. I knew she was telling me George's blood pressure was rising. I said, "Let's take a break for a bit for coffee." Connie went straight into the kitchen and started to brew a large pot.

Julie and I met in the kitchen. She told me George's blood pressure was rising, especially on the last question, and his hands were starting to shake more violently. "A sign of alcohol withdrawal," she said. "And he wants to stop the questioning."

I told Julie that what really happened when Lenny died had to be disclosed now or we may never know just what happened. Theresa Marie came into the kitchen and Julie asked her if she had any of George's medicine with her. She said yes, she always carried some just in case. Julie instructed Theresa Marie to give George his pill and to keep the bottle handy.

When she returned and Connie joined us, I confided to the girls. "We are at a crossroads with George. If I continue, I might have to get rough verbally with him to disclose what happened. His risk of a heart attack or a stroke was real. However, if I could get George to tell or acknowledge what really happened, his recovery from being alcohol dependent could be greatly improved. Theresa Marie, as spouse, and Julie with her medical knowledge, and myself were the three people who had to decide what to do. Two no votes and we stop now, or two yes votes and we continue on. "Let's have some coffee first and not make a snap decision," I suggested. "Thumbs up for yes and thumbs down for no when we are ready to vote."

Julie returned to the dining room with two cups of coffee, one for George and one for herself. She took his vitals again. I pulled my chair off to the side, away from George, in hopes he might relax; which he seemed to be doing. We all seemed to relax a little as we sat around the table not speaking much.

When my coffee was finished, I said, "Vote."

Three hands rose with three thumbs up. I asked for a Bible and Connie put one on George's lap. We would proceed and hope for the best.

I got out of my chair and slid it in front of George. Theresa Marie sat on it, grasped both her hands around George's free hand, bent forward, and told him to try to remember what happened when Lenny was killed—not what he thought had happened. "This is the only way you can hope to recover from alcoholism," she said. "I love you so very much. Us asking you to tell us, is showing how much we love you." She gave George a long kiss on his forehead and a big hug before she stepped aside for me to sit down.

I asked Connie to clear everything off the table except the recorder and I sat down in front of George. "Can you tell us what led up to the accident?" I asked.

For the first time since the barn, George spoke. "Lenny and I stopped to empty the combine grain bins into Connie's grain trailers and she headed for the granary with them. Lenny climbed into his combine and started the engine—but I had to have some whiskey, so I called out for him to take a break. He couldn't hear me over the engine noise so I waved my arms to attract his attention. He saw me but still couldn't hear me, so he got out of the combine and we met in front of the running combine away from the engine noise in back." He paused and took a deep breath. "I told Lenny I had to go to the barn to take a break. Lenny said no. I was out of whiskey and had to have a drink quick. So I told him again and he answered, 'Just one more hopper full, then we can break for chores and supper. We can finish the last of the field after supper.' George stopped talking and his face froze.

Julie twisted her hand into a thumbs down direction which I knew was a bad sign. I blurted out, "You didn't just give Lenny a poke—you punched him in the chest and knocked him backward into the revolving blades of the combine, didn't you?"

"Stop it!" George yelled back. "I didn't mean to hit him so hard. And then he was caught in the blades and the safety clutch on the blades disengaged and I ran and turned off the combine. Lenny was caught up in the blades and was bleeding from the throat ..." George broke down. His entire body was shaking, tears were running down his face, and saliva began flooding from his mouth.

Julie yelled, "Call 911 and tell them possible heart attack, stat! An emergency nurse is attending, but without any drugs. Tell the dispatcher to have the doctor on the pill bottle call Julie McGregor stat. Give her my cell phone number.

"Guys, help me get George on the table with a pillow and blanket. She tore open George's shirt and pulled it off his body. Phil and I raised George onto the table and laid him flat. A couch pillow appeared from nowhere, and Julie yelled for a cold, wet towel which was put on his forehead. Julie was busy with the blood pressure cuff. Theresa Marie and Connie were to remove George's shoes and trousers and to cover him up with a blanket.

Phil and I ran to the vehicles to move them out of the way for the expected ambulance. I said I would flag down the ambulance and Phil should go inside and help Julie. It seemed like an eternity, but in seven minutes the ambulance was backing up toward the doorway. Julie was on her cell phone with George's doctor and wanted to know if the EMTs had a certain drug. They said they weren't authorized to carry it in the ambulance. The doctor told Julie to give George three of the prescribed pills and also three aspirin. He should chew them if possible. It was a struggle to get the pills into George, but finally he did swallow them. George was transferred onto the gurney and strapped in and covered with blankets. The EMTs wasted no motion and had him out the door and in the ambulance. I looked at my watch. Only eleven minutes had elapsed since the 911 call was placed. Efficiency and teamwork was at its best this day.

The five of us were still standing by the table when I picked up the blanket that had covered George. I was going to fold it up. With the blanket in hand, I froze for an instant. Someone had emptied George's pockets and put his stuff on the table next to the Bible. A silver St. Christopher medal lay next to the open Bible, with the page showing the following entry:

> Presented to
> Lenny McGregor
> On his tenth birthday
> May 24, 1960
> by
> His Father and Mother
> Dennis and Eileen McGregor
> David City, Nebraska

"Everybody, look at what page the Bible is opened to and the medal next to it," I said.

They all saw the inscription and the medal, then made the sign of the cross. We all hugged each other, so we were all in a tight gathering. Someone started reciting the Lord's Prayer and everybody joined in. When we finished the prayer and opened our eyes the Bible was closed. We all stood in amazement. The Bible had closed on its own while we prayed.

Connie said, "There were seven of us gathered here today—six humans and Lenny's spirit looking over us. He brought us companionship, nourishment, music in our hearts, and the guidance to set everything straight on how he died. I think most of all he was looking after his brother George. Everything will be for the best."

"Amen to that," we said.

I looked at Phil and said, "It's time for your leadership of the families. What would you like us to do?"

"The first priority is getting Theresa Marie to the hospital and get George registered in. Julie, you take her to the hospital in her truck. Connie, you take Trev to George's house and show him where everything is so he can start on the chores.

Then return here and do your chores and clean up the mess we made today. Then go back to George's and finish helping Trev. When the work is done, come to my house and we will go to the hospital together, that way everybody has a ride home. Trev, I'll help you load George's drum set into your Suburban.

"When I get home, the first thing I'm going to do is contact Mark, a college buddy of mine who's a criminal attorney in Lincoln. I want to set up a meeting in David City to consider the legal implications for George. The quicker we notify the sheriff, the better it will look for George. Mark owes me a bigtime favor and I'm going to call in that marker.

"I know Mark," Julie said, "because he comes and visits with us. He's a gentle soul but can be tough when he needs to."

"You know best Phil," said Theresa Marie. "Just do it. George has committed a crime and he must be represented by legal counsel."

With that, we all set about going our separate ways.

~ ~ ~

Connie and I pulled into Phil's driveway as he was coming out of the barn. "Do you guys smell like cows?" he asked.

We answered yes and we all laughed.

"Let's wash our hands and faces before going to the hospital. I want them to know we are working people from the country—sort of giving a good impression, you know."

I thought to myself that Phil has a dry wit about him and smiled.

After our mini cleanup was done, we left for the hospital.

Chapter 26

THERESA MARIE AND JULIE MET US IN THE LOBBY. They told us George was stabilized and any chance of him having had a heart attack or stroke was slim. His strong physical condition made the difference between something good or bad happening. Theresa asked how we got through the chores and we replied, "One cow at a time." She knew she had no worries about her livestock.

The girls gathered together in a corner while Phil and I found chairs off to one side. We were engaged in light conversation. "I have two things to put to you, if you want to hear them," I started. "First, I can stay longer, until you line up some help with Theresa Marie's livestock. Your whole family has treated me like one of your own, and no price tag can be put on that."

"You are welcome anytime, for as long as you want to stay," replied Phil. "And the other thing is?"

"It's a lot more complex and not very well thought out. That's where you fit in perfectly," I said. Phil looked puzzled, but said nothing. "Phil, I get funny feelings lately, and I can't explain them. Like the Bible closing by itself today. Usually something pleasant happens when I get them, sometimes not so good. The feeling I'm getting now is sort of a dull nagging feeling—and it concerns the farms. Like everyone, we concern ourselves with weather in one- to three-day periods and not the long-term forecast. My inner thoughts seem to be with crop failure due to drought in the Central Plains, where we are. I get these little flashes or images of all things, windmills, lots of windmills. Can you make any sense of that?" I asked.

Phil didn't smile or laugh or scowl or frown. He just stared off into space.

I felt bad for suggesting another problem for his family; especially with George's problem. "I should just shut up and not be a nuisance," I apologized.

Phil came to attention and said, "No. You just unlocked my brain from hidden memories. "Let me tell you a story that I had long since forgotten. When my brothers and I were young kids, we found all kinds of ways to entertain ourselves. One thing we liked to do was climb in trees or jump from the top of the roof in the barn into the cushion of the hay mow. The climbing was as much fun as jumping. My dad had bought a used windmill and pounded down a well and installed a windmill near Mom's garden. Dad told her that when we had a power outage we would still have fresh water from the windmill well. We used to climb that windmill all the time. We could watch the storm fronts coming toward us.

"From you seeing windmills in your thoughts, I recalled Dad measuring the amount of time it took for the windmill to fill two buckets with water. Just now I realized he was doing an experiment on how much water per minute and dumping the water in a ten-foot square area and the depth in the soil the water would soak. He always carried a stubby pencil in his pocket that he called his pocket calculator. He would scribble numbers and determine how long it would take to water an acre of land to one inch of soaking. While he would be scribbling, us three kids would climb the windmill tower and pretend we were pirates on a ship. We used to yell like sailors we saw in the movies. We had a great time up high in the air.

"I remember Dad put that windmill next to Mother's vegetable garden. He put an old leaky garden hose from the windmill and ran it along a row of the garden. Every couple feet or so he would cut a small slit in the hose. We climbed down from the tower and watched Dad release the brake on the windmill and soon water was coming out of the slits in the hose. The wind was probably blowing normal that first day; soon the water was squirting out of the slits. He went back to the barn and returned with another old hose and attached it to the first hose and then cut slits in it, too; then he stood back and watched. We thought this was great because we didn't have to carry water to Mom's garden anymore.

"I remember Dad saying something like, 'How about that kids?' He then went back to the barn and returned with four more hoses and attached them to the ones already in the garden. We all stood back and watched the water from the slits slow to a seep then stop altogether. We yelled at Dad that the water wasn't coming out anymore and he had broken it. He smiled at us and said, 'Let's just wait a bit and see if they start leaking again.'

"Dad sat down in one of the two chairs he had put by the well, filled his pipe, lit the pipe, and sat down to wait. We three kids kept going to the hoses looking for water. After a while, water started coming out of all of the slits and us kids jumped for joy. He hadn't broken the watering system after all. Dad told us to get Mom so he could show her his new invention. 'And tell her to bring some cookies for us,' he added. Mom came back with us, carrying a pitcher of lemonade and we brought the glasses and cookies. That was the best afternoon, eating fresh cookies with lemonade and Mom and Dad watching the water seep around her vegetables.

"Sometime after that, one of us kids asked Dad what we should call his new watering system. He replied, 'Irrigation.' Irrigation was a new word for us but we soon knew it a whole lot better because Dad kept drilling new wells and windmills all along the edge of the fields, each being spaced just so far apart. Soon the neighbor kids started calling our farm 'Windmill City.'

"That summer was hot and dry, and a lot of the neighbors' crops were nearly dying from lack of water, while Dad's were doing fine because of the water from the windmills. The neighboring farmers quit kidding Dad about all of his windmills.

"Eventually Dad took down the windmills, disassembled them, and they're stored in the old barn. When he drilled all those field wells, he left a threaded joint about fifteen inches below the surface and put steel caps on the well heads. All three farms have wells in place. Some of mine are six to eight inches in diameter. Dad made detailed maps of all the wells locations, their depth to water, and the size and length of every well on the three farms. They should all be workable; all we need are velocity pumps and electricity. The only equipment we need are pumps and pipe for overhead irrigation; then we could irrigate to our hearts' content.

"Your comment about windmills may save us from a lost crop this year, or future years for that matter," Phil finished.

The girls came over to Phil and me, wanting to know what we were jabbering about so intensely. Phil replied that he would have a special job for all of them soon enough and they should be ready to work in the fields all day for a while.

Connie said, "Now, wait a minute. Just because the tractor is broken down doesn't mean I'm going to be a horse and pull a plow."

"Oh, no," Phil assured her with a smile. "Just a lot of walking and a bit of shoveling here and there."

"I can tell you guys are up to no good and us girls are going to pay the penalty," Julie said to Phil. "I haven't seen that devilish smile on your face in a long time."

Theresa Marie asked, "Does this have something to do with Dad's boxes in the attic?"

"Sure does," answered Phil.

Connie asked Theresa Marie if she had any idea what was in the boxes. She said no.

It's hard to tell how far the conversation would have continued because a doctor came into the waiting room with a report on George. He reported that with the medication George was now asleep, his blood pressure had dropped to a safe level, and his shaking was almost gone; although it might come on strong again over the next couple of days but not to worry. The night staff was appraised of his condition and he was to be called at any time should there be a need. So far, George was doing great, even better than he had hoped for. He would check George out first thing in the morning. He said we should go home and get some rest. We all felt relief from the good news and thanked him for his caring help.

Chapter 27

THERESA MARIE, JULIE, PHIL, AND CONNIE HAD A meeting scheduled with Mark, the attorney, at ten the next morning.

Connie and I were both dragging our feet when we got up. It was going to be another long and stressful day for the McGregors and they didn't need me getting in their way; so I told Connie to take her time and I would take care of all the morning chores. I could tell her mind wasn't on the farm work, but rather on what was going to happen with George. She went to take a hot shower and I headed to the barn.

I had milked and fed all the livestock and chickens when I stepped into the kitchen. Connie looked refreshed as she finished preparing breakfast for us. She asked how Bessie was doing and I said another one and a half pails this morning.

Connie said it was almost time for her to leave and I should change my clothes. I replied that I would only be in the way. The meeting should only concern the family. I would stay here and start work on some of the equipment. She understood and nodded approval. Before she left, I handed my tape recorder to her.

All forenoon and afternoon my mind was on George and

what was going to happen to him after the meeting with Mark. Being an officer of the court, Mark would have to notify the sheriff and maybe the county prosecutor, which meant George would be arrested and charged with a crime. From that point on, it was anybody's guess what would happen.

Even though I kept myself busy in the barns, the day dragged. About four-thirty, Connie pulled into the yard. When I first heard her car, I dropped my tools and headed to meet her. I caught up with her as she was entering the kitchen. I started to make a pot of coffee while she headed for a dining room chair. I so desperately wanted to ask her how the meeting went, but I kept my mouth shut, knowing she would inform me when she was more fully composed.

I filled two mugs with the fresh coffee and put one in front of her and gently started to massage her shoulders and neck. Those muscles were tight, like bowstrings. Connie sighed with pleasure as I massaged; gradually a lot of the tension started to go away. She raised a hand and placed it on mine. "That feels so good, don't stop," she said. "I'll tell you what happened in a minute."

Chapter 28

"WHEN WE ALL MET IN THE HOSPITAL LOBBY, I handed the attorney your recorder. Phil informed Mark that George had admitted accidentally killing Lenny. Phil said he had arranged for the use of a conference room and we should go there.

"'George is an alcoholic,' Phil said after everyone was seated at the large conference table. 'Which was the cause of Lennie's death.' Phil pointed to the recorder and said it was all on the recorder and it would tell Mark the whole, sad story. Mark turned on the recorder and listened to every word. Mark had lost the jovial smile he had when he entered the lobby. Now it was all business as he spoke to all of us.

"'I am an officer of the court and it is my duty to inform the sheriff of this new disclosure. What shape is George in?' he asked.

"'Not good,' Phil answered. 'He's in withdrawal and awake, but under heavy sedation. Not coherent at all. He just wants a drink.'

"Mark said, 'Phil, I am a recovering alcoholic. Mine started innocently enough at the university, when I would go out with my friends and have a couple of drinks before studying. The harder the courses, the more I drank. Although I didn't know it, I was on the fast track to becoming fully addictive. My job can be very stressful, and the more stressful the case, the more I wanted a drink.

"'Sometimes in court, my condition would be so bad I could feel my hands shake and I couldn't think clearly so I would have to ask the judge for a recess on some dumb excuse. I was lying to the judge, for God's sake! Somehow, I became friends with a guy named Jacky. He started riding herd on me, until one day I lost complete control and he took me to the hospital.

"'The hospital staff knew what was wrong with me and called my parents, who knew nothing about my alcoholism. My parents got me into a rehab center and I spent six months drying out and trying to get my life back together. My wife never knew of the problem either, and from that first day in the hospital, she has done everything she can to keep me away from booze. She takes care of me like a mother hen with her chicks. Some recovering alcoholics dry out in days, and others never do. Loving, family support and prayer help the best in recovery, but an alcoholic is one for life and is never fully cured. I am also a diabetic, which makes alcoholism even worse; so I am on guard 24/7 and do a lot of silent praying.

"'How your family treats George can make a big difference in his recovery. That quizzing on the tape was a work of art. Whoever he is, I wish he was on my staff. For him to get George to admit in one sitting is truly amazing. Many interrogators only get part of the story and some never do, no matter how hard they try.'

"Mark then said he wanted to talk with George, to explain what has to be done. Julie left to ask a nurse. When Julie returned she said that Mark could talk with George for a few moments, but she would have to be present. That being said, Mark and Julie went to George's room. Upon entering, Mark talked in a very pleasant voice and told George he was in trouble with the law. George nodded and said he knew. He asked what would happen. Mark explained he would meet with the sheriff as soon as possible. George said, 'Do it now, times a wasting' and slumped back into his pillow. Julie checked him over and his vitals were holding steady. Julie told the duty nurse that they were done seeing George and returned to the conference room.

"Mark went outside to phone the prosecutor. He returned a few minutes later and said we had to get right over to the courthouse because an immediate meeting was to be held. When we were all seated in the prosecutor's Mark said this meeting concerns the death of Lenny McGregor. New evidence pertaining to it happened yesterday and that a crime had been committed by George McGregor. Mark slid the recorder to the prosecutor and stated that the recording on the tape reveals the whole truth of the crime and that he and the sheriff should hear it as evidence.

"We all sat in silence as the tape played to its conclusion. The sheriff removed the recording chip and placed it in an envelope. The sheriff asked where George was. 'In the hospital drying out and under sedation,' answered Julie. 'And just who are you?' asked the prosecutor. 'I'm an emergency nurse at the hospital and a sister-in-law of George. George shouldn't be removed from hospital care under his intoxicated condition.'

"The sheriff then said he would have George arrested on a homicide charge and a Deputy Sheriff would be placed outside of George's room at all times. The prosecutor excused himself and went into another office. When he returned he said a judge would hear our charges against George now, in

Courtroom #2. We all entered the courtroom. Mark handed the clerk a quickly drafted form and the clerk read: 'George McGregor, charges second degree manslaughter.' She passed the form to the judge. 'Where's Mr. McGregor?' The sheriff answered, "In detox center for alcoholism. He is too unstable to be present at this time.' Mark said, 'Your honor, please. I am the attorney representing George McGregor and he pleads guilty to the charge. A tape in evidence disclosing the crime has been turned over to the sheriff. It establishes no intent and that the crime committed was accidental, mainly due to the intoxicated state of George McGregor.'

"The judge ruled, 'I therefore assign this case to be held one week from today at 10:00 a.m. at which time George McGregor will be present. Case closed until the 7th of March 2016.' And the judge banged his gavel."

Connie asked me what I thought would happen. I replied a number of different verdicts were possible, either good or bad for George. The judge could rule harshly because a lie had been made at the inquest of Lenny, and three years had elapsed with the truth hidden. On the other hand, if the judge listens to the tape and realizes the circumstance of George's life, he might give a lighter sentence. George will not get off scot-free and will have to pay a penalty. There is a strong possibility of jail time but I didn't think it would serve any good. A lengthy probation and community service might be assessed; that's the best punishment George can expect I supposed.

"I know your mind is spent but would you like to take a slow stroll around the farm a while?" I asked.

She said, "Yes, it might help to clear my head from the heartache I have."

When we returned, Connie asked me "How do you know when to ask me to do the best thing at the right time?

I would have just gone in the house and plumped down in a chair and brooded all night. I feel much better now, thank you."

I didn't reply.

We sat there for some time before I remarked that Theresa Marie should not call her children until Connie and Julie had a chance to talk with her. The last thing George needed was disruption. His kids could do more harm by their concern and actions than could be gained by their presence. If she called them, she should ask them not to come home yet, but wait until later, when George was stable enough to have his family around him.

Connie agreed so she called Julie. Julie said she would call Theresa Marie now and the three of them would get together in the morning to discuss the problem further. Apparently Julie's call came just as Theresa Marie was about to phone her kids and tell them what had happened. She agreed not to call tonight, and the three would get together in the morning to discuss what to do.

My trip had turned into a real mess of an adventure, with no clear-cut solution. I didn't want to walk out on them and leave them to their struggles. But, I did need to return home to take care of my own necessities. I would drive to Phil's tomorrow to see if a working plan could be arrived at.

Chapter 29

THE NEXT MORNING, CONNIE AND I AWOKE TO A thunderstorm. The rain was sorely needed and it would be three weeks before any more would fall.

Connie and Julie went to talk with Theresa Marie while Phil and I sat down to work out a plan on repairing Connie's equipment and how I could best fit into the work schedule. We concluded that the first two implements to be worked on were the tractor and disc. The tractor was of major concern because we didn't know how much damage was done to the engine.

Phil said he had never worked on the internal parts of an engine and was at a loss of where to begin. I said I felt comfortable working on the engine but we shouldn't run the engine. The tractor should be towed into Lennie's garage.

"I'm sick from thinking how bad it could be," stated Phil.

"Don't be yet," I said. "We might get lucky and find everything is acceptable.

"Were you a mechanic at one time?" he asked.

"No, but I had auto mechanics #1 and #2 in college as part of my Industrial Arts major. I have also pulled a Chevy

350 engine and replaced a crank shaft in a Chevy van without pulling the engine in my pole barn," I said.

Phil poured us two mugs of hot, strong, leftover coffee and we went to his equipment barn. I started circling each machine slowly. "Your equipment looks in great shape," I stated.

"Thank you," he said.

When the rain stopped, it was a mild day so we sat down outside the barn in lawn chairs. We talked over the equipment situation at some length. I told Phil he needed to lay out a plan for us to follow as to the order of repair of the equipment and I had to return to Northport to take care of some stuff. I would be gone about two weeks. When I returned, I could stay as long as it took to get everything fixed, if he wanted the help.

"You know stuff I don't. We want you and need you very much. We already think of you as part of our family," said Phil.

"Okay, that's settled then. I'll leave tomorrow morning. When I return, I'll teach you everything I know. For me, books are great for learning something new, but doing a job with your hands and mind stays with me better and longer."

"Yes, sir. Mr. Sherlock," Phi said, and we both laughed.

Our nicknames would keep us loose during the tasks before us.

Chapter 30

THERESA MARIE, CONNIE, AND JULIE DECIDED THAT Theresa Marie should call her daughter Ann, and son, Joe. She would ask them not to come home until after George was better and knew the penalties he had to face.

When Ann's response was uncaring, Theresa's built up tension exploded and she ripped into her daughter about not coming home since Lenny's funeral. About the only mail she received was a preprinted Christmas card and if she called, at most it was only twice a year. "You've turned into somebody I no longer know and you don't care about anybody but yourself. You don't even think to bring my grandchildren here to spend the summer. If Momma Eileen was here, she would shake you up and paddle your butt till you couldn't stand it any longer. You just sit out there and feed me that crap about how much work you have to do and the parties that you attend. Well, I tell you we are in a disastrous situation, and you say 'So what?' And on top of that, your brother is worse than you are, if that's possible.

"Don't come around here until you get your head on straight, because if you don't, your kids will be worse than you are. And don't come crying back to your father and me until you clear it with me. I've had it with you. You're nothing but a cheap, selfish snob. Goodbye!" Theresa Marie hung up the phone, burst into tears, ran into her bedroom, and slammed the door shut.

Connie and Julie went into Theresa's bedroom and tried to console her. Theresa Marie had said almost exactly what was in the back of their minds about their own kids, who had been behaving just like Theresa Marie's.

The phone rang and Julie answered it. It was Ann calling back to talk with her mother. Julie blew up at her niece. She told Ann her mother was crying her heart out over her treatment over the last three years. "And, on top of that, Connie's and my kids are just like you. We ought to disinherit all of you and give the farms to the church in spite. If you want to do something, phone your cousins and tell them what kind of assholes you all are and don't deserve any consideration or forgiveness. Goodbye!" Julie said and hung up the phone.

When Connie stopped at Phil's house and told him what had happened, she was still fuming. Julie was taking Theresa Marie to the hospital to see George and wouldn't return home until Theresa Marie was ready to leave. We all agreed that George should never learn of the blow up that occurred that day.

It was very quiet on our ride home and afterward in the house. Finally, to break the ice, I told Connie that Phil had worked out a plan where I would return to Michigan, get my business taken care of, and return in two weeks. I would be leaving in the morning. I admitted it was bad timing, but if she could hang in until I returned, I would make it up to her some way.

Thankfully Connie recognized the fix I was in and said she would welcome me with open arms when I returned.

That night as we were both heading to bed, Connie

stopped me and asked if I would sleep next to her. She needed me close for one night. I was taken by total surprise and, although it wasn't right, there was no way I could turn her down. I took Connie in my arms and gave her a big, long hug and asked if she was sure. She murmured, "Only until 6:00 a.m."

The next morning at six we both arose and dressed for the day. She asked me to do the chores one last time and she'd fix me the best travel breakfast ever. When I returned from chores, Connie had filled a full size dinner plate with an omelet that had mushrooms, bacon, sausage, and a lot of other stuff I couldn't identify. She put it in front of me with a glass of freshly squeezed orange juice, toast with grape jelly, and a mug of fresh brewed coffee. I gave her a thank-you hug and remarked that with this feast I would put on ten pounds and Susie would be leaning to the left all the way home.

She remarked, "You deserve every morsel for what you have done for us in the last few days. Bessie is going to miss you too."

"Please keep your cell phone handy," I said. "When I stop to take a break, I'll call you and let you know where I'm at and how the trip is going."

She replied, "I would like that very much."

Chapter 31

THE FIRST DAY I STOPPED ABOUT EVERY 100 MILES TO stretch my legs and to keep my back muscles from cramping; and, of course, to give Connie a quick call to keep her up to date. The phone never rang more than twice. I think she was timing my distance to how long it would take. I told her about what I was seeing and how the traffic was going and the backup of traffic in the metro areas. She once remarked that she felt like she was riding with me.

I told Connie I was going to call my friend Elaine in Iowa City to see if I could spend the night. She turned ninety in January and was on the go all the time. We were usually in contact with each other once a week to keeping each other up to date. During my travels, I had slipped to calling her every two weeks, although Elaine didn't mind because I had all the more stories to tell when we did talk.

Elaine said she had a bed for me. I took her out to her favorite restaurant and really caught up on everything that had happened in our lives the last three months. Her three kids had all got together and threw a big birthday party for her in January. She had lots of pictures of her kids, grandkids, and at least fifty of her friends that made the trip. Those who couldn't attend the party called her on the phone and she said by the end of the day she was worn out.

The following morning, Elaine and I had a good breakfast. I would be at my home in Northport in about eleven hours. On the way, I would make a quick stop in Kalamazoo to visit Kay's grave.

The visit to the gravesite wasn't the happiest because our combination marker had not yet been laid and the manager at the cemetery gave me a big song and dance about how bad the winter had been and they had at least sixty headstones to lay and ours would be done in due time. I had gone around and around with him in making Kay's funeral arrangements and he acted like an egotistical snob and tried to make the arrangements as difficult as possible. Everything was supposed to have been taken care of in our pre-arrangement contract and we had checked with him twice to be sure everything was in order and paid for. After charging my credit card $750 for additional overpriced charges, the burial date was set. I stormed out of his office having had to deal with him for an hour and a half.

I was mad and it was now too late to continue my drive home. I called one of my wife's first cousins and made arrangements to stay at the Shook's farm in Fulton. Another cousin said he would contact the other five cousins living in the area and we would all get together for dinner in Vicksburg that evening at 7:00. Another family that doesn't need an excuse to get together. A dinner to be spent with close relatives and a place to stay for the night. I told them of the situation in Nebraska and that I would be returning to help them out.

The Shooks had all been raised as farm kids on the old homestead and their parents had purchased another farm nearby, totaling about 200 acres. When I told them that my new friends in Nebraska had 5,000 acres on each farm it about blew them away. Jokingly I remarked that would be a lot of pickles to pick. Instantly there was an uproar in discontent. One cousin spoke right up and said she could hardly think of a pickle much less eat one. The other cousins firmly agreed.

I had brought back unpleasant memories for all of them. I recalled the situation. Their father, Bob, had planted a large field near the house with pickles as part of his crop rotation and it was the children's job, all ten of them, to pick pickles each day, all summer, until school started and then he would plow them under. Those ten kids picked pickles six days a week all summer whether they liked it or not because the revenue was needed toward paying the property taxes and some of the income toward their college education. Bob also bought about fifty calves as feeder cattle for the kids to raise and care for. Some of that income was also placed in the fund for their education. Those accumulated funds paid for a university education for all ten kids. All of the kids told their father never to plant pickles again or they would all leave home. Bob never planted pickles again! All of them graduated with different major and hold responsible employment in their field of knowledge. A joyful and happy family that knew how to work and play. After dinner with the gang, l went to the farm to settle in for the night. One cousin had turned on the furnace and pump and had the farmhouse ready when I got there.

Connie and I had a lengthy conversation that night. I filled her in on the problem with the cemetery guy and the story about the pickle ordeal for the Shook kids. Connie asked how big a field were the pickles in and would guess five to six acres. She about blew the receiver off my ear when she heard the acreage and started to laugh hard and loud. When she finally got enough control, she said it really wasn't funny. Those poor kids picking all those pickles on their summer vacation! "My mother once planted six pickle plants in her vegetable garden and I spent every day picking pickles from those six plants, but five acres—my god, that had to be horrible!"

The next morning, I stopped at a nearby cousin's and bummed a cup of coffee and a bagel and hit the road. I gassed up Susie and called Connie. I told her I was on the road again and to allow about six hours as I had to gas up and get groceries before I would get to my house. She asked if there was a lot of snow and I answered a little in shady spots, but the highway was clear and dry. "As I drive north, though, I will start to see a lot more snow, and by the time I reach Northport there could be anywhere from eight to fifteen inches on the ground. Even with my garden tractor blower it will take about five hours for me to clear the driveways."

She thought that was terrible having so much snow to deal with and I chuckled that it was really fun blowing as long as the tractor or blower didn't break down.

We signed off and I continued my drive north.

Chapter 32

SNOW, SNOW, SNOW.

There hadn't been a lot of melt off so far and although spring wasn't too far off, the Canadian north wind and the temperature of Lake Michigan were having their normal effect on this part of the state. Our spring weather was almost always two to three weeks later than in Southern Michigan, which is why cherries and other fruits do so well as it delays the budding process and lessening the possibility of frost damage.

Trudging through twelve inches of packed snow, I open the door to my house. It was a comfortable 50 degrees inside. The furnace had worked perfectly at my thermostat setting. I turned up the thermostat to 68 degrees, the water pump, and after a few minutes the water heater. There was a dial tone on the phone and I needed to call the county senior services to set up an appointment to have my taxes done by their volunteer. After making that call and another to their tax volunteer person, my appointment for next week was made. I then called Connie and told her I was home and everything was in order. I would be spending the rest of the afternoon blowing the hard-packed snow from my two driveways. I said goodbye to her and got into my snow-blowing garb and trudged through the snow to the pole barn to get my tractor blowers. The tractor batteries had to be reconnected and hopefully they had enough charge remaining after being idle for so long.

A quick shot of starting fluid to the antique Bolens tractor and after about four tries it fired off and ran smoothly. This tractor has a single-stage blower and would grind its way through packed snow and ice and would throw the snow twenty-five feet away. I put a battery charger on the battery of the other tractor and then set about getting the snow removed from the driveways and the road leading up to the drives. This would be a three to four-hour job, but I felt good about doing it. It was great to be back home and not living out of a suitcase for at least a couple of weeks.

The next few days, I did lots of puttering and collecting items to take with me to David City. I sorted through the box of junk mail and put two grocery bags of it aside to drop off at the recycle center. There had be at least $50 worth of postage wasted on this mail, not counting the cost of the special paper used and the fees the commercial artist and printing companies would have charged. The Post Office says it needs this bulk mail in order to survive and with it they keep raising the postage rate almost every year.

I set out tools I thought would be needed, namely my torque wrench, impact sockets, and impact gun. I called Phil and addressed him as Dr. Watson. We started our conversation with hearty laughter. He said from time to time Connie and Theresa Marie would address him as Dr. Watson; so I must have told them our inside joke. I told Phil not to buy a torque wrench because I was bringing mine. He filled me in on the planning for the repairs and said he had made out a worksheet for each field regarding the location of all the wells Dennis had drilled.

He said Connie would fill me in on George's trial when I talked with her. She wanted to tell me the good news and could hardly contain herself. George must have gotten a break from the judge.

Phil then told me of his problem with his septic system and asked for my input. Just what you don't need is a pile of shxx to go with all the other problems he had to deal with. I asked him when was it last pumped out and he said never by him. I told him he had an expensive problem to correct and he would have to hire the job out. He asked why.

"All three of the farms were built about the same time, and George's and Connie's septic systems will probably fail in the near future. When the house was built, it was a common practice to use steel tanks as septic tanks and dry wells, and in time the bottoms and sides rust out. The septic tank then emits raw sewage into the soil and can, in time, contaminate your drinking water. If the surface soil is receding where the tank and cesspools are located, it is a sure sign they are no good and need to be replaced. That's a job for an excavating contractor."

I told Phil to find a reliable contractor to quote him a price and if it sounded reasonable ask him if you could get a quantity discount if he did the three houses. "Make a deal if you can. Figure about $6,000 for each system. Call your local health department for site inspections, what they require on size requirements, and new placement locations. Let the water level recede to handle gray water and activate your outdoor Johnny and slop jars for the other necessities. It will be like camping out for a while.

Unless you want to pay twice to have your tank pumped I suggest you hold off until you see when the contractor can start. If that's too long a time, then have it pumped out now.

"Julie will be congenial about so long, so get things started tomorrow and explain the situation to her. I'll inform Connie of the situation and you can tell George and Theresa Marie. All of you can then decide what action to take—but you have to do your system, regardless.

"Another thing is older systems have cast iron pipe inside the house and then extend usually just outside the foundation wall where they convert to clay piping to the septic tank. In your new system, put in your contract that Schedule 40 4" sewer pipe replaces the old clay tile pipe. Also, health departments want tile fields used instead of cesspools so figure an area of thirty by fifty feet for a tile field location where there are no trees or shrubs. Put a stake where you would like the new field for the Health Department man to accept. Also the new septic tank and field must be at least fifty feet from your water well and he will not allow any exception. How does that grab you?" I asked.

"I don't feel too red hot now, except under the collar."

"Sorry, Dr. Watson," I said and we ended our phone call.

I phoned Connie. She told me the scheduled date for the trial and that George would put himself to the mercy of the court and hope for the best. The sentencing would occur at a later date. I told Connie about Phil's septic problem and I recommended she have hers replaced also. She said she would tell Phil to include her system in his negotiations with the excavator and health department. The next day, George approved his system so all three homes would have new updated systems and there would be no future problems on sewage for any of them.

Eight days had elapsed since leaving Nebraska and I was ready to pack Susie and head to David City for at least four months. In a way, I was sad to leave home, but the need to help them and their friendship would make it all worthwhile.

PART III

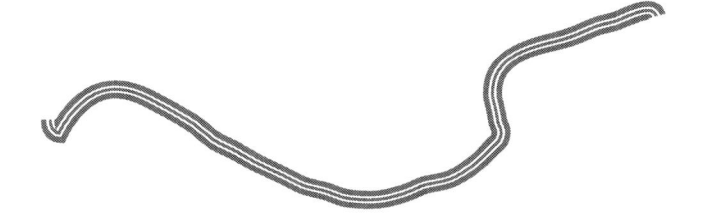

Chapter 33

I WAS PACKING SUSIE TO START ON THE ROAD IN THE morning when the phone rang. Another political survey or some politician I thought as I looked at the caller ID and it said unknown caller. Another junk call waiting to bug me. I answered it anyway and a lady on the other end of the line introduced herself as Ann the daughter of Theresa Marie McGregor. She was calling from California. She wanted to know if I was the Trevor Jones who was a friend of Theresa's. I replied yes. She hurriedly said, "Please, don't hang up. I need your help."

"What's your problem?"

"I'm desperate because my mother won't answer my calls and I can't communicate with her at all. She won't answer calls from my brother either. I called my cousins and told them how terrible we had all been and Connie and Julie won't answer calls from any of them either. If any of us go to see our parents, we know our parents will slam the door in our face. There's eight of us and our parents will have nothing to do with us and it's absolutely terrible. We just don't know where to turn or what we can do.

"I remembered I still had a note from Mother saying

there was a new friend of the family and he was doing a lot to help all of them through their problems. Mother really gave me hell, which I deserved. Maybe she told you about her blow up—but before that, she mentioned your name in the note and that you were from Northport, and through the Internet is how I found you."

"When all three realized they felt the same way about how they had been treated by their kids, they simply realized all of you didn't give a damn about them and it wasn't worth the continued grief in trying to deal with it. All you kids cut out your parents from your lives and turnabout is fair play. You say you feel bad because for the last week or so you have been totally ignored. All you kids have ignored them for years. How would you feel if you were ignored for years?"

Ann was quiet, then replied, "The same way."

I continued. "So you feel remorse or worse—but for how long? Just until the problem goes away or are you going to stick with it for the rest of your life and really want to be a loving part of her life? All of you took a so-what attitude and that's what got you in this fix. There is one slim possibility that loving feelings can be restored, but I don't know that I can put my trust in what you really want to do.

"How far are you willing to go? Just around the block or circle the earth for eternity? You have to do something, show something, or say something so I can believe in you and believe what you want to happen. I know what your answer should be, but I don't believe you have correctly thought out the problem. You tell me."

"I really don't know what else I can say," Ann said.

"Your answer is hidden in what I have said to you tonight. If you've really been listening to what I have said, the answer will come to you in big, bold print." I gave her my cell phone number and said, "If you or your husband can't figure it out, then call your cousins and relay what I have said. If none of you can realize what the answer is, then there isn't much hope for establishing a lasting parent-child relationship. Search the Bible, you may find the answer there. When one of you finally figures it out, call me on my cell phone any time, night or day, and I will tell you a possible way to re-establish a relationship.

"All of you are well-educated persons, but you can't see the forest for the trees. Look beyond what you are seeing now or look into your childhood as to how it was between you and your parents. For now, I think this conversation is at an end. I'll be ready for your call," I said and we hung up.

I went to bed hoping to get a good night's rest. I was sound asleep when the bedside phone rang. I rolled over and removed the receiver from the cradle, pulling the cradle off the nightstand. It banged onto the floor. I mumbled hello and a lady identified herself as Angie, a daughter of Connie McGregor. "You said we could call night or day."

I told Angie she had woken me up and I was in a stupor. She said she had talked with Ann, her cousin, earlier. Although stymied for a solution, Angie had gone to bed and was sound asleep when her mind snapped her awake. "I sat up in bed with a jerk," she explained. "Pulled the covers off my husband, and woke him up. He asked me what was the matter. I told him I now knew what I needed to do, how to act, and what to think. My subconscious mind told me to do for my mother first and myself and others afterward. All this last week and for years before, it had always been me first and everyone else later. I've been a fool or worse—and I'm going to start changing now, this very day. I'm sorry to ruin your sleep, but I had to tell you, so that I can heal."

I said, "Your mother and her sisters-in-law never mentioned their children's names to me. I believe they were ashamed to. We all know why, don't we?"

"Putting myself in her place, I can now understand why they all feel like they do toward us," Angie admitted. "But now they have removed us from their lives and I don't know how or where to start."

I was becoming more alert. "You've already started to heal and I will work with you toward additional recovery, but you will have to realize the answers to my questions. First, what is your education, or employment if you have a job?"

She answered, "I graduated from U of Nebraska and have a master's degree in Public Education. Now, I teach English in high school; previously I taught at the elementary level."

"Good," I said. "You have just the right background to use in your recovery. Once you have a grasp of how you need to think, you can be the tutor for the rest of the family. You have me wide awake and I need my morning coffee; maybe you also need yours. Let's leave the phone line open while we get our brew. We are going to stay connected and get answers and a possible solution, no matter how long it takes."

We both put down the receivers and made some coffee.

We resumed our conversation. "Think, now," I said. "As your mother, what would you think? Your children have cut you out of their lives and you feel despair. You don't care about what goes on with your daughter and sons."

"Okay," she replied.

"What is the important thing you are missing?"

"I don't know."

"Think, Angie." No answer. "When you were teaching elementary students and your class or the school put on a program for the parents, who could you always count on being there, besides the parent or parents?"

A pause, then she replied, "The children's grandparents."

"Bingo," I replied. "Who always makes sure a child gets a birthday card with a little money or a nice present? You take away that caring love and you have a very unhappy grandmother or grandfather. So, what is your answer?"

"I can forget about my kids but I miss my grandchildren terribly."

"As a parent of grandchildren, how do you reconnect with your mother?"

"Through my children," she replied.

"Now, I hope you understand your mom's feelings and your aunts' and uncles' as well. Their desire for a relationship with their grandchildren is the crack in the doorway to them. If you go very carefully, you will possibly work your way back into her graces. How to go about it, is where it gets tricky.

"Use your creativity in doing the following. Talk with your children about their grandmother; discuss what she likes to do or her interests; what you remember from your childhood, like when your mom played with you and things she would make for you, like clothes for your Barbie doll. Develop your kids' interest in Grandma and how wonderful she treated you as a child. Give examples if you can. Get your kids' interested in your mother so they want to reach out to her. Ask if they would like to write a letter to Grandma telling her about an activity they are engaged in. Maybe they want to ask how she is doing on the farm. Have them address the envelope to Grandma McGregor, and you fill in the return address with your child's name. Your mother might not open a letter from you, but I guarantee she will open a letter from her grandchild. If the child's letter asks a question, your mother will send a return letter, for sure.

"Don't send a whole bunch of things at once. Space them out so your mother will feel the children want to do this on their own. A school paper, clippings, church or school photographs, etc. Search through your kids' closets with them and suggest that Grandma might be interested in something; have your child mail it to her. Don't rush into enclosing a note that your child would like to visit the farm during the summer. Don't press, just suggest and see what happens. By this time, your mother will want to see her grandchildren, at least on the farm. Pray that you are doing the right thing at the right time.

"The situation today developed over time—and it will take time to return to a normal condition. Work with your siblings and cousins on this. Take baby steps and maybe your mothers will respond to you. 'Love you' and 'Miss you' are excellent closings to your notes."

After absorbing what I had said, Angie took a breath and then asked, "What is the disaster Theresa Marie and my mom mentioned?"

"The short version is your uncle George is an alcoholic and when your father died it was because George wanted to stop working to get a drink but your dad wanted to make one more trip around the field. George got mad and lost control. He punched your dad into the rotating blades of the combine, causing his death. After disclosing this information, George has been through detox, was charged with manslaughter, and been sentenced.

"Since your dad's death, no maintenance has been done on your mom's farm equipment. Your uncle Phil thought George had done the maintenance because George told him he had. So now all of your mother's machinery is a disaster and if it can't be repaired, it could cost $500,000 to replace."

The phone line was quiet except for sobbing and occasional voices in the background. After several minutes, Angie asked if I was still on the phone. I replied, "Yes."

"Every one of us McGregor kids is to blame—and not just Uncle George. If we had visited home, we might have noticed Uncle George's drinking habits and done something about it. Now my dad is dead, the equipment is a total loss, and poor George is guilty of manslaughter—all because we stopped caring for our parents. Trevor, thank you so much for confiding in me. I'll keep you informed about what we are doing."

I told Angie I was departing that morning to return to David City, gave her my cell phone number, and requested that only Ann or she call me. We said our goodbyes and hung up.

Chapter 34

I WAS FAIRLY WELL RESTED AND READY TO GET ON the road. I called Connie to tell her I was leaving and, if I didn't get tired, I might drive all the way nonstop. It was 926 miles to David City and would take eighteen hours, allowing for gas stops and fast-food eateries. Most of the route was on I-80, and if I needed a break there were usually rest stops about every 100 miles. Connie told me to be careful and not to overdo it. Sound advice.

The biggest problem I would face was driving around Chicago and the heavy traffic. Around metro areas, many people act like they are on a speedway and drive as fast as they can, cutting in and out of traffic. I've found that a steady cruising speed at the posted limit is the best way to travel. Many motorists travel ten miles over the limit and a constant check in the rearview mirror is a must or you might get run over or have them blowing their horn for you to get out of their way. Many times, following a semi at a slower speed works well, but they block your view for posted lane directions. Sometimes you can't win no matter what you do.

At about 400 miles, I looked for a place where I could

stop to fill Susie's gas tank, get something to eat, and stretch my legs. Iowa would be the next state I crossed. Thank goodness I was far away from the northern snow country, and I now had dry pavement.

As I neared Nebraska, dusk was coming on and my eyes were getting tired; so I decided to pull off at the next rest area to gas up, get a bite to eat, and then stretch out flat in the back of Susie to rest for a spell. I called Connie and told her what my plan was. She gave out a sigh of relief. It's wonderful to have somebody who cares about your well-being. That's one of the things I liked about Connie. I felt lucky to have such a wonderful friend as her. I told her I would call before I got back on the road. She appreciated my keeping her up to date, and now she could relax knowing I was off the highway.

Rest stops are a wonderful idea, except for the coming and going of semi-trucks that never turn off their diesel engines. Rest is the correct word to describe the stops because that's all anyone can expect to get. To fall asleep in a rest area is next to impossible, and that was all I got was a rest. I closed my eyes for two hours and felt refreshed and ready to head out on the last leg of the trip. I phoned Connie and told her to expect me about 1:00 a.m. and to have a fresh glass of Bessie's milk and some cookies ready when I arrived. I asked how Bessie was doing and Connie replied she was back to three-quarters of a pail of milk. She missed me. The two hogs were also suffering because they weren't getting the extra milk that Bessie had been giving. I thought it was something when a cow misses a human being. It wouldn't be long and Bessie and I would re-connect.

As I drove around Omaha, I knew I would soon be back at my second home and hugging Connie. I realized how much I missed her and, even though a lot of hard work was waiting for me, I knew there would be a lot of very happy times with the McGregors.

As I drove through David City, I noticed the town was almost deserted. I pulled off to the side of the road and gave Connie one last call and told her to turn on the yard light. Except for no snow, entering Connie's yard would almost be like it was in March when Susie had broken down—except this time I knew who would be opening the farmhouse door.

I can't describe the marvelous greeting I received from Connie (of course, I returned the favor). While I enjoyed the cookies and milk, instead of sitting across from me, Connie sat down next to me. She felt that was where she belonged. Needless to say, I was pleased with that change.

Chapter 35

I GOT UP AT 6:00 A.M. AND FOUND CONNIE IN THE kitchen, getting ready to go to the barn to do chores. She was surprised to see me up so early. "Chore time and Bessie waiting for me," I said.

"You drove almost one thousand miles and only got four and a half hours of sleep and you are up to do chores. For heaven's sake, go back to bed," Connie said.

I told her I was going to do the chores and that I wanted a home-cooked breakfast instead of the fast food I had on the drive here. I grabbed two 2 pails and headed for the barn.

I gave Bessie a good rub around her head and ears, pitched hay into her feeding trough, freshened her water, and gave her two sugar cubes. Then I went to her stanchion to start the milking. She took a look at me and continued eating the hay. One pail was full and another three quarters full when I was finally done. I released her from the stanchion and she started nuzzling my hand. I told her I had only brought the two sugar cubes but she could have some oats, which I got for her. I cupped my hands together full of oats and she licked them clean, wagged her tail, and headed for the barn door to the barnyard. I had spoiled her before and she was taking advantage of it. She acted more like a pet dog than a cow.

I entered the kitchen with the two pails of milk and Connie stared at them and shook her head. She mumbled something about me and that cow, but I couldn't understand everything she said. She had the table all set for breakfast and was busy at the stove while I put the fresh milk in the fridge and washed up. I had just turned on the radio for the morning farm report when Connie entered the dining room with a platter full of big sausage patties, pancakes, fried eggs over lightly like I liked them, and enough strips of bacon to feed four people. I said, "Why so much food?"

With an impish smile she said, "I'm going to get you so full of food, you will have to take a nap."

"You have everything here except steak and potatoes," I declared as I started to load up my plate.

"Steak and potatoes are for tomorrow," she said.

She ate her normal amount of food while, I admit, I made a pig of myself.

While feasting on this great breakfast, I remembered when I was about eight years and my brother and I were staying at our grandparents' farm in Ann Arbor for the summer. My grandmother was an excellent cook and her pancake batter was her own recipe and the sugar syrup was also her recipe. It wasn't as thick as the syrup you can buy at the grocery store today. Her pancakes were also about half as thick as the average pancake mixes are today.

One morning at breakfast, my brother and I must have had a hunger tantrum because we kept emptying the pancake platter looking for more, and Grandmother made another batch several times. When we finally had our fill, Grandmother remarked, "I never had two kids eat so many pancakes in my life. You two boys must have eaten at least five dozen pancakes! My brother and I never ate that many at one sitting again, although Grandmother did make up a double batch for the rest of the summer.

I didn't want to be a total fool and ask Connie where the orange juice and coffee were, which was good because without me saying a word, she brought two fresh mugs of coffee to the table and sat down beside me. She asked if I had enjoyed my trip back to Northport. I told her that I had missed her, I sure hadn't had any meals like she had just served us, and that the last of the snow would probably be gone in three weeks.

"Three weeks!" she exclaimed. "It's springtime here and flowers are popping up all over. How can you stand such long winters?"

"One day at a time," I said. "However, the bonus is, we don't have mosquitoes when snow is still on the ground."

She said, "You're pulling my leg and just stringing me along."

"No, I'm not stringing you along. This was a light winter, actually, as Northport only had 125 inches of snow. A hard winter is when we get 235 inches and the snow stays until almost Memorial Day."

I couldn't convince her I was telling the truth. We had almost finished our coffee when Theresa Marie, Phil, and Julie pulled into the yard. I saw Phil's face light up when he spotted Susie. They all entered the kitchen and I, with a serious face, told them to stomp the snow off of their boots. They all said there wasn't any snow out there; it had all melted in March. "Not in Northport," I said. "There was still six inches on the exposed areas and two feet in the shady areas."

Connie jumped in and said, "He's been feeding that

garbage to me half the morning and I don't believe a word he says."

I was going to shrug it off but instead said, "Phil, pull up the Weather Channel for Northport and see what it says."

Phil studied his smart phone, looked up, and said, "Forecast is for two to four inches of snow and the temperature is 26 degrees. The total accumulation for the week will be between ten and twelve inches. How in the world can you grow anything up there?"

"We have fruit trees, mostly cherry and apple. The cold Lake Michigan water keeps the buds from forming too early and over sixty percent of the tart cherries that are grown in the U.S. are grown in my two-county area."

They couldn't believe it was still snowing in Northern Michigan because it was shirt weather this morning and the temperature was expected to be in the middle 70s.

Julie said, "No wonder you drink coffee all the time—just to stay thawed out!"

Phil and I figured out a work plan for the day. The girls would start locating the wells Dennis had installed years before, I was to work on the tractor engine, and Phil would work on the disc plow. We all left Connie's house to carry out the orders of the day.

The girls and Phil left with the ATV while I went to the shop and found Connie's tractor set up for me to start figuring out just how bad of a condition it was in. Phil returned a little later and found me under the tractor engine removing oil pan bolts. I had two loose pan bolts left when I asked him to help me lower the oil pan so no oil would spill on the floor. Each of us held up one end of the pan and the last two bolts were removed. Using two screwdrivers to slightly pry the pan loose from the engine, we lowered the pan to the floor and slid it out from under the tractor.

Phil had a five-gallon bucket ready and we poured the oil into it. There was at least three fourths of an inch of solid carbon-oil sludge in the bottom of the pan. That was not a good sign. The oil pump screen was almost plugged shut, and the chances of salvaging the engine were next to nil. Sludge stuck to everything in the crankcase. Phil and I were discouraged. I told Phil to get me the tube of Plasti-gauge while I removed the flywheel cover and took another pail and a roll of paper towels sitting on the floor. I grabbed the flywheel; rotating it to the point of least resistance; and, with paper towel in hand, checked to see if there was any play on the connecting rod journals, one at a time. Phil intently studied me and the rods as I did each one.

I said, "So far, they felt okay." I removed the rod-bearing cap for cylinder #1, wiped the journal clean, and gave it a close eyeball inspection. Next, the bearing in the cap was wiped clean and inspected for scouring. "So far, okay on #1 rod," I said. As I put a bead of Plasti-gauge on the journal and reinstalled the bearing and cap, I asked Phil to bring me my torque wrench. I torqued the rod bolts to factory spec, then removed the nuts and bearing cap. From the Plasti-gauge packaging directions I determined that rod was within tolerance. I reinstalled the bearing and cap and finger-tightened the nuts and continued doing the same on each rod until they were all checked. I rolled out from under the tractor and cleaned my hand. I could tell Phil was dying to hear my verdict. I again said, "So far, so good." I could see the tension release in his face and shoulders. "Let's take a break and see how the girls are doing locating the wells."

We went to the ATV and headed toward the field where they were working. "There's one well we can't find," said Julie.

Phil examined the drawing he had made and remembered that particular well. On Dennis's drawing there was a smudged measurement and the figure Phil had written down was his interpretation. He raised his head and said the measurement was his fault. He was about twenty to twenty-five feet off. He picked up the metal detector and started backtracking while the rest of us watched. After about twenty feet, he stopped and began a back and forth motion with the detector. "This should be it," he said. One of the girls grabbed a marking stick and handed it and a mallet to Phil. Phil and I both praised the girls for the progress they had made, then we returned to the tractor to continue checking the crankshaft.

The main bearing had four bolts instead of two so it took a little longer to check the clearance on each bearing. After the last bearing checked out okay, I yelled, "Hurrah!" and breathed a sigh of relief.

We both got out from under the tractor and gave a high five—but no back slapping as our hands were covered black with sludge.

It was about lunchtime, so we cleaned our hands and arms and went after the girls. When we got to them, they started laughing. Phil and I didn't know why. They finally said the two of us looked like warriors. Phil and I looked at each other and started to laugh too. Black sludge smeared our faces.

We all returned to the house for lunch—although Phil and I made another stop at the parts cleaning tub first.

It was time to start chores. Even though the girls had been hard at work, walking up and down the fields wearing heavy farm shoes on soft soil, we said it was time for them to take a needed rest. Phil and I had been lying on our backs most of the day and had a lot of energy left—but

SAMARITAN ADVENTURER

those three wonderful ladies were determined to tough it out, doing what would normally be a man's job. We all went to the dining room, where the girls fell into their chairs like a ton of bricks. Phil and I went into the kitchen to make a fresh pot of coffee.

Suddenly the phone rang; quite a few times before Connie lifted the receiver. It was Mark, the attorney in Lincoln. He asked to talk with Theresa Marie. Connie handed the receiver to Theresa Marie. She spoke to Mark and said, "Not another postponement." Mark said that he had just received a call from the Court. Sentencing was to be held at ten o'clock the next morning. She was to be there and see that George had a fresh suit of clothes to wear. Theresa Marie said she had his best Sunday suit and shirt and tie already ironed and laid out for him. She would take them to the jail this evening. She agreed to meet Mark at the courthouse before ten o'clock tomorrow.

Connie hadn't yet returned to her chair when the phone rang again. "What now? Nobody ever calls me, except you guys or some solicitor wanting me to donate money or to have me buy their garbage." She picked up the receiver. It was the excavation contractor from David City who said they would be at her place early tomorrow to install the new septic system if was okay with her. She replied, "Do it. Start any time after six."

After Connie hung up the receiver, Phil asked her what that was all about. Connie said the new septic system would be installed tomorrow. "Great timing," she remarked, "as we will all be in town for George's sentencing and we will be out of their way."

I asked Phil how his septic system problem worked out. Phil replied that the system was just as I had described. The contractor had the new system installed in one day.

The next morning, trucks and equipment started arriving just after six. A sod cutting machine started cutting sod while the heavier equipment was unloaded. Men were rolling up the freshly cut sod, large tarps were spread out on the lawn, and a backhoe started digging for the sewer line at the house. Things were really popping by the time Connie left for the courthouse.

I had asked the owner when Theresa Marie's system was scheduled. He asked if I meant George McGregor and I nodded yes. He replied he couldn't reach them on the phone and no one was home. He wanted to do it tomorrow. I answered I was sort of their agent and he had my okay to start tomorrow. He said he would store some equipment there overnight and that would save a lot of time and money.

I returned to the repair shop and reinstalled the oil pan and added a quart of General Motors Engine Cleaner, a new oil filter, and fresh oil to the engine. Phil had already replaced the valve cover gasket and had painted the valve cover and air cleaner. The engine looked great. Checking further, I saw that Phil had replaced the fuel injectors, the brake master cylinder was to the full level, the power steering and hydraulic reservoirs were full, and the engine was ready to start up for a test run. Before I turned the ignition, I realized that Phil should be the one to start it. He would know of any quirks in starting the engine and if the sound of the engine was normal.

Next I checked the cab enclosure and lightly sanded all surfaces that I wanted to repaint. That done, and still no word about George; so I wiped all of the painted areas with Prep Sol and started to mask off areas that weren't to be painted. I heard the excavator's trucks running and saw some of them heading for town and the other equipment

SAMARITAN ADVENTURER

heading toward George and Theresa Marie's. I inspected the work they had done. It was a beautiful job.

Connie pulled into the yard and I went to the mailbox. We met somewhere between her auto and the house. The first feature I noticed was her smile from ear to ear. I handed her the mail and we walked hip to hip into the kitchen where she started a fresh brew of coffee and then looked through her mail.

I was dying to know how the sentencing came out and she was teasing by delaying telling me. I bit my tongue and took the cookie jar and put it on the dining room table in front of where we would be sitting. Her eyes were gleaming with delight and she was staring at an envelope that was in this day's mail. I realized she was going to tell me the results like I tell my stories: insert suspense and delay the results to the very end of the story.

One envelope had her full attention. She took a knife and opened the envelope, removing a piece of wide-lined paper. She carefully unfolded it and began to read. I picked up the envelope. It was addressed to Grandma McGregor in a child's writing and a neatly printed address, city, state, and zip code. The return address was printed by a child named Sally Anderson, with neatly printed address, city, state, and zip code below. I later read the letter. Sally wrote that she liked to draw and her mom had said you had lot of animals.

> I drew these for you. A Goat. A cow. A horse. A dog. Hope you like them. Love you.
> SALLY ANDERSON

Connie's eyes started to blur as she re-read the letter and passed her fingers slowly over the drawings. She got up, went into the sitting room, and returned with a box of Kleenex. She already had several in her hand and re-read the note again. With a choking voice she said the letter was from her granddaughter Sally, her daughter Angie's little girl. "This letter is the first one I ever received from a grandchild. I'll treasure it the rest of my life," Connie said. "I'm going to put it on the refrigerator door." I handed her the envelope and she placed it beside the letter.

There are times when a guy should keep his mouth shut and this was one of them. Knowledge of George's fate could wait. This was a very special moment for Connie and I wasn't about to spoil it. Over and over she would pick up the letter and pass her fingers over it, then suddenly she picked up the letter and envelope and smelled them both and a smile came to her face and she smelled them again. I just sat back and watched her carefully fondle the letter. This simple letter with drawings would forever be her prized keepsake.

Suddenly she jumped up, went to the phone, punched in a phone number, and exclaimed, "I just got the most wonderful surprise from my granddaughter Sally." It was Theresa Marie on the other end. Theresa Marie must have asked Connie three times for Connie to re-read the letter. Connie was too excited to sit down and just kept walking around the dining room with the long phone cord dangling along behind.

I wanted Connie to enjoy this special moment; so I went into the kitchen and got the two milk pails, showed them to her, and headed for the barn. I learned later that when Connie ended her conversation with Theresa Marie, she called Julie and the whole episode played out again.

I had milked Bessie, given her a treat, let her out in the barnyard, and was cleaning up the milking parlor when

Connie appeared. She was so full of joy and excitement, she was simply bubbling all over. To her that letter was a million-dollar treasure and it only cost forty-nine cents to mail. She came over to me and gave me a big, long kiss on the lips and thanked me for letting her experience her time of joy without interruption. We each grabbed a pail of fresh milk and returned to the house.

From that day on, Connie kept a lookout for the mail lady and they had a talk and Connie told her about the special letter she had received. The mail lady said if she saw a letter addressed to her by a child's handwriting she would give two long blasts on her horn.

The next day, Theresa Marie and Julie received letters from their grandchildren—and the excitement happened again. When the girls got together to locate more wells, most of their conversation was about the letters they had received. Of course, the letters were passed amongst them. These three ladies were in heaven, so to speak.

Oh, yes. What about George and his sentence?

Connie was having a lot of fun; so I said I'd wait while she figured out just how she was going to tell me the story. When Connie was ready, this is the story she shared:

"When we met Mark outside the courtroom, workmen were coming and going from the courtroom. A deputy came to us and said that there was an electrical problem and the workmen were trying to fix it. The courtroom should be ready by one o'clock, but no guarantees.

"George was still locked in his cell and the only people that could see him were his attorney and his wife. Theresa Marie decided to wait with George. Phil, Julie, and I drove over to Walmart. For three hours we walked every aisle and every single department, including the toy department and the pharmacy.

"When we returned to the courthouse, we were told the courtroom would open shortly before 1:30 p.m. When we entered the courtroom, we sat behind the defense table. George was already there, and the handcuffs were removed from his wrists. He turned around and told Theresa Marie that this was his day of reconciliation and he was going to take it like his father would, as a true Scotsman would. He turned back toward the judge's bench and seemed to be staring at the American flag in total silence; sometimes bowing his head. Finally, the court clerk read the order of business and the charges facing George and the judge ordered George McGregor to please rise and to face the judge.

"The judge began—and I hope I get this right—'This court has deliberated long and hard in arriving at a just penalty for the crime you have committed. I have considered your dedication to your church, to the 4H program that you have supported for many years, and the assistance you have given to the County Agricultural Department and never having a misdemeanor or crime on your record until now. You surrendered to the County Sheriff upon acknowledgement of your crime. Alcohol was given to you as a young lad and it became a way of life to you, but you didn't realize what it was doing to you and these things all enter into my decision.

"'The ruling of this court is as follows: You are to serve three years in imprisonment with three years credited as served, which is the length of time you suffered from the time of your brother's death; two years of probation, reporting monthly to your probation officer; 1,000 hours of community service to be completed before the end of your probation. To attend AA meetings at least every two weeks; and the total cost of repairing or replacing the neglected and misused agricultural equipment owned by Mrs. Connie McGregor is to be paid in full by you to her satisfaction. Violation of any of these penalties will automatically rescind the three-year time credited provision and you will then serve three years in custody at a penal institution.'

"George whispered something to Mark and Mark addressed the judge. 'Your honor, the defendant wishes me to convey a message to this court.' 'Continue,' said the judge. 'Mr. McGregor wishes to thank the court for the benevolence and kindness in your ruling.'

"The judge closed the hearing, banged his gavel, and returned to his chambers. George hugged Theresa Marie for the longest time and then George turned to us. He said, 'I can't believe the kindness extended to me this day. Every day I will extend a kindness to whomever I meet or needs help. I know I will need help every day of my life to fight off my addiction, and I would like all of you to be my mentor.' Then the tears flowed from all of us.

"George is a different person. He has a humbleness that I never saw in the twenty some years I've known him." "I think George is going to start a new story, completely different from his life so far," I said. "And we can help him in so many little ways, starting with a big one called love. He needs all the loving help we can give him."

Chapter 36

THE NEXT DAY, EVERYBODY MET AT CONNIE'S FOR the work program for the day. For the first time in many years, George was a happy man and wanted to do whatever was assigned him. He was a changed person. No more grouchiness, he bubbled with enthusiasm and a raring-to-go attitude.

The girls had one farm left, George's; they would have their lunch break there. George was assigned to clean and restore the seed planting machine. Phil brought his tractor to Connie's to give it a cleaning with the pressure washer, recheck it for any possible repairs, and get it ready for a new paint job. I would finish masking Connie's tractor and give it a new paint job.

Later in the afternoon, when the girls returned, we would surprise Connie by showing her a bright shiny tractor. She didn't know anything about the paint job. I had purchased a stick-on letter kit that had gold letters on a black background. I would apply "CONNIE" on the doors below the windows so her tractor would be personalized with her name.

I finished masking, mixed up the new paint, and opened

both sliding doors to the workshop for cross ventilation. Everything in the shop was covered with old bedsheets or blankets. I loaded the spray gun and worked off a plank stretched between two step ladders, started painting the roof of the tractor and repeating it on the other side and finished doing the roof. I refilled the spray gun and started painting the front, back, and both sides. It was a beautiful "Case Yellow," but very dull.

I walked over to George. The back of his shirt was all sweaty. When he turned and saw me, he tried to straighten full upright with difficulty. The front of his clothes were soaking wet from both his perspiration and the spray from the pressure washer. I gave him a good laugh. He said, "Boy, am I out of condition!"

"Too much sitting and not enough doing," I said with a chuckle. "How's the cleanup coming?"

"Very slowly," he replied. "Some knucklehead didn't do his job like he was taught and that knucklehead is paying for it now."

I returned to my project. The color coat of paint had dried rapidly in the warm air. I inspected every inch of the surface and lightly sanded the paint. Then, with a clean lint-free cloth, I wiped the surface with Prep-Sol cleaner. I emptied and cleaned the spray gun and loaded it with the Clear Coat and sprayed everything again. The clear coat really made the Case Yellow glitter and shine.

By now, George was finished with his project. After we changed into clean clothes, I said it looked like the shop had aired out. "Let's go inside and remove the masking tape before the girls return. When they get here, you can present Connie with her "new" tractor. When George said he hadn't done hardly anything to repair the tractor, I replied, "You're paying the tab, old fellow."

He nodded in the affirmative and we went into the maintenance shop and removed the masking tape. George grabbed a spray bottle of glass cleaner and a roll of paper towels and started cleaning all of the windows, headlights and taillights while I replaced the "Slow Moving Vehicle" sign on the rear of the tractor.

That being done, we both stood back and admired that beautiful tractor. A brand-new tractor didn't compare to the appearance of Connie's tractor. I handed George some of the letter kit and he applied "Connie" to the door on one side and I did the same to the other door.

I heard the ATV down the road, heading our way. It was the girls returning. I said to George, "Move the tractor into the daylight and I will bring the girls to see what has been accomplished."

On my way to meet the girls, I heard the most beautiful sound of that diesel engine starting and smoothly idling. I greeted the girls as Phil pulled into the yard with his tractor. I led all of them to the maintenance garage and there stood the glistening tractor. "A present to you, Connie, from all of us," I said.

At first she just gazed at the tractor, but then at a dead run went to it and rubbed the paint lightly and walked around and around it and hugged each one of us.

George took Connie's hands and said, "All of us present you with your new look-alike tractor, with your name on each door."

Connie kept wiping tears of joy from her cheeks and she hugged all of us again. George asked if she would like to take a test drive and she replied, "Can I?"

George opened the door to the cab for her to get inside. He closed the door and stood back as Connie started the engine, put it in gear, and drove it onto the highway. When

George turned toward us, his eyes, cheeks, and the front of his shirt were wet. He was deeply touched and came to each of us saying thank you and embracing us at the same time.

A short while later, Connie returned, with the tractor running at about three-quarters throttle. She parked it in the equipment barn and gleamed with delight. We all gathered in a tight group and embraced each other. I broke the silence by saying I would check the mailbox. That brought everybody to attention and they headed for the farmhouse. Phil ran to his tractor, grabbed a box, and yelled, "I have a box from Jimmy and it says I have to open it in front of all of you!"

There was no special mail for Connie this day, but there was a surprise package for Phil. Phil set the box in the middle of the table while the girls made two pots of coffee. As we waited for the brewing coffee, Phil, George, and all of the girls took turns picking up the box and shaking it a little. What could be so special that his grandson wanted all of us, and especially Phil, to enjoy?

Finally, the coffee was ready, the mugs were filled, and Theresa Marie handed the box to Phil. We all waited impatiently as Phil slit the tape and folded back the flaps. A letter was on top. It said to read this letter first before removing the contents.

The letter, addressed to Phil, read something like this:

Dear Grandpa Phil,
I like to run all the time. I run 4 miles before breakfast, two miles during our lunch hour at school and I have joined the track team and run everything except cross country and run all the way home as the school buses have all left.
I don't run after dinner because I need to do my

homework. I do this every day of school and on the weekend after my chores are done for the day I run 10 miles to build endurance. There is one boy a grade ahead of me that I just can't seem to beat. Sometimes I get close to winning but I always come in second. Maybe that's why I keep trying, I don't know. He's my best friend in school and we pal around a lot and sometimes run together on the weekends.

Someday I'm going to beat him and I think he will be happy that I'm getting better. My mother got on my case a week ago and insisted that I clean out my stinking closet and get rid of the junk stashed on the floor. I threw away a lot of old stuff that was worn out and was no longer of any use to anybody including my brothers. There was one favorite item I couldn't part with until I thought of you and I decided to give them to you so you might think of me the same I think of you. You may now examine the contents of the box and then return to my letter.

All of us had our attention glued on Phil as he carefully unwrapped the item, which turned out to be an old pair of running shoes enclosed in a plastic zip lock baggie. We first gasped and then broke into the longest burst of laughter, that would subdue a little and then burst out again. There was coughing, choking, and arms and hands grasping our stomachs while leaning over the table. It was a long time before anyone could speak. Phil returned to the letter:

The stink in my closet was from my favorite stinky shoes and you can see I really wore them out good. I put them in a plastic bag so the Post Office wouldn't reject my mailing them to you. If you do keep them I hope *they will remind you of me and I would like something that I might remember you by.*

Love you, Granddad.
Jimmy

P. S. Mom put two air wicks in my closet and told me to leave the door open so the closet would air out.

Phil opened the baggie a little and quickly zipped it shut. "Phew!" he said and handed the bag to Julie, who passed it on to the next person. The rest of us opened the bag and quickly closed it with the strangest looks on our faces. I made the remark that if Phil was smart, he would hang the shoes in the hog pen and let that aroma sweeten up the smell. They all agreed and we burst into laughter again. That ended the saga of the stinky shoes, and they hung in the hog pen for a long time before Julie allowed them in the house.

All of us were fatigued. As our gathering ended, each of us knew this had been a memorable day, affecting all of our lives for the better. I think Lenny and God were with us every moment.

Chapter 37

IN THE DAYS AND WEEKS THAT FOLLOWED, THE SIX of us worked as a team. The well extensions were ready to be connected to portable pumps mounted on four carts with generators. The fields were ready for planting by the girls, each driving a tractor with their name on a door, and George was busy as a beaver repairing the equipment that would be needed as the weeks went by. One field on each of the farm had been planted last fall with winter wheat and those were left as is. Appropriate fields had hay seed, oats, soy beans, and corn in the ground ready to grow.

Hardly any rain had fallen and the fields were too dry for the seeds to germinate so the guys hooked up the wells and overhead irrigation began. Phil recorded the moisture of every field daily and entered the readings in a log. The moisture readings were important to know how much watering to do. Too much water and the soil would compact hard around the seedlings and have poor root structure and the plants wouldn't develop properly or even cause the seed to rot. Too little water and the seeds wouldn't germinate.

Each daybreak Phil walked the fields, testing for moisture and, when everybody would gather, he would assign a crew of two to each field requiring irrigation. Some days George would be in David City doing public service. Before returning, he would do the grocery shopping for the girls. In time, the cashiers, mostly women, got to know George and enjoyed his constant chatter on most any subject. We received feedback that that former grouch was really a nice guy after all. That made us all happy, especially Theresa Marie.

The crops were doing great and Phil and George kept a close watch on the winter wheat that would soon be ready for its first cutting. Because of the irrigation, all of the crops were more advanced than the adjoining neighbors'. The McGregors would be the first to cut hay.

The neighboring farmers would stop by the fields for close examination and walk away with envy. Their fields hadn't been irrigated and were doing poorly. And at this time, they could do nothing to correct it.

In our group planning sessions and on Sunday afternoons after dinner, the demise of the neighbors often came up. We felt bad their crops were failing because of lack of rain. About two days before the hay cutting was to begin, George said that we were doing so well and our neighbors so poorly, that we needed to help them out somehow. It was decided that since we had three very large hayfields to harvest, and it was too much for the six of us, even if we worked fourteen-hours a day, we could hire some of our neighbors and their hay balers to give us a hand for pay. We could use three more balers and a crew to load the bales onto wagons and transport them to the storage barns. From her records, Connie told us how much money we could devote to the extra help and Phil and George would make the offer to the closest neighbors that evening. George remarked that being a good neighbor to a neighbor in need was good therapy for him. We chimed in that it was good for us too.

It was arranged that at 10:00 a.m. the machinery would start to roll with six balers steadily winding up and down the fields being trailed by hay wagons and guys slinging the bales on the wagons. A break for lunch and everything started up again. The hired neighbors were elated to have something to do and when the day ended, although tired, there were smiles all around. The next day, the operation would be repeated until the harvesting was completed and the neighbors would take their equipment to our next farm.

Connie logged in the number of bales stored in the barn and at days' end had a total that had been harvested. That evening after dinner, she announced the total bale figure and it was a record yield per acre for that field. Phil and George were amazed and, of course, very happy that all of the hard work and irrigation with God's help had made it possible. After all, three farms had completed the hay harvest, the storage barns were stacked to the rafters with the baled hay, and the first cutting had been completed.

Because of the drought, crop yields in Nebraska would be way below normal and a shortage of hay with higher selling prices would have an adverse effect on the milk producers and feeder cattle operations. Many farmers, aware of the bad situation, started selling off some of their livestock at a lower price because the market was glutted with way more than normal cattle being auctioned off and sold. Those farmers were between a rock and a hard place.

Again, George raised the question that although we had to make a living and show a good profit for our labors, we shouldn't take advantage of the people that really had it tough. Connie again came to the rescue by telling us what the average price of hay was in prior years and what the asking price was this year. There was a large spread of prices. The number of bales of hay required for George's and Phil's livestock was computed and the surplus bales would be sold direct to the livestock farmers at a price slightly larger than prior years' averages. That plan was agreed by all and it would be fair to the buyers and to us as growers. There was to be no greed involved in this plan; it would be fair to all. We all felt it was a Godly thing to do.

Chapter 38

IT WAS THE MIDDLE OF JUNE. WE WERE ON TOP of the world with everything going smoothly; so it was decided that a day off from the work would be in order. Everybody but me had catching up to do. Connie was off to town. George wanted to do public service and check in with his probation officer. And Julie and Theresa Marie set about cleaning their neglected homes.

I had nothing in particular to do, so I put a rope around Bessie's neck and went for a stroll down a road that was next to a cornfield. Bessie acted like, and I treated her like, a pet dog. Together we happily walked along the shoulder of the road. We had walked a short distance when I started to get that strange feeling again. It had been months since it had last occurred; so it was a surprise to me.

As the two of us walked, occasionally I would go to the corn and look at the beautiful green leaves. The farther we walked, the stronger the feeling became. Suddenly I felt a strong urge to examine the corn more closely. The leaves, though beautifully formed, had thin, tiny whitish streaks on them. I didn't like what I saw so I decided to turn around and take Bessie back to the barnyard.

While at the barnyard, I called Phil and Julie's home. Julie answered and I asked to speak with Phil. She said Phil was out in the barn doing something and she would have him call me. A few minutes later, my cell phone rang. I said hello and Phil said, "Hallow, Mr. Sherlock. What can I do for you today?"

I replied, "Dr. Holmes, I have something I think you should look at right now."

I couldn't explain what I had seen, other than I thought something was wrong. I said he should bring plastic gloves and some large baggies. He didn't ask why and said he would be right over.

About ten minutes later, he pulled into the yard where I was waiting with the ATV. He got in with a puzzled look on his face, and I drove us down the road to the cornfield where Bessie and I had been. We got out of the ATV and I pointed to the cornstalks that had streaks on their leaves.

Phil bent over, put on the plastic gloves, and on his hands and knees, he started twisting the leaves in different directions, eyeing them very closely. He stood up and walked in different directions from that spot, pulling leaves from various stalks and placing them in individual baggies as he did so. He returned to where I was standing by the ATV. With a troubled look on his face, he said, "We have a bad problem. The corn has the start of a virus infection, and it could be serious." He explained that at the State Ag meeting he attended last winter, it was disclosed that there was a new strain of virus that was very difficult to treat and chemical manufacturers were trying to come up with a treatment. The two different viruses looked almost the same to the naked eye; and it took a super microscope to detect one from the other. He would call U of Nebraska chemist in the laboratory and inform them that he was sending bagged samples from his farm for identification on overnight FedEx.

We returned to the farm, got into his car, and drove straight to the FedEx office, where the samples were packaged and mailed.

That being done, we went to Burger King and drank a shake as he explained the two viruses and the effect they would have on the corn. One strain was treatable and the other one was still in research for a cure. A little success on treatment in some cases, but nothing positive so far. Even though the shakes were good, he did not look happy. Many of the corn farmers were not aware of the two strains of virus and would spend time and money treating something that was untreatable. He wasn't going to guess which virus was on the corn; that's why he sent the samples to Lincoln. Now it was wait and see until the lab got back to him.

I asked if something like bleach or vegetable oil would slow the development until a treatment was developed. He didn't know the answer to that question. "How widespread is our infection?"

He replied, "Very small now but it will spread because of wind and water."

"Ouch," I said. "In this dry weather, the corn needs irrigation. If we stop irrigating, we lose the crop." He nodded in agreement. I suggested we pull the affected plants out by their roots and place them in plastic garbage bags until an analysis was completed. He agreed. We stopped at the local hardware store and bought every last box of 45-gallon garbage bags and a roll of plant twist ties and headed to his place.

With plastic gloves and a small shovel, Phil and I dug and removed every infected plant we could find and placed them in the garbage bags and double tied the tops of each bag. We used his pickup truck to hold the filled bags. When we finished, he called George and Connie and told them there was an emergency meeting at Connie's at eight o'clock that evening.

He dropped me off at Connie's and told me to change my clothes and to have Connie wash them in extra-strong soap with double rinses, and that I was to place the clothes in the washer and for her not to touch them until they had been washed. He was going to do the same when he got home.

When Phil got home, he changed his clothes, washed his face and arms in strong anti-bacterial soap, and then phoned the State Ag Department. He pumped them for all of the information they had on the virus and had them fax whatever they could to him.

At the meeting, Phil placed one plastic bag with an infected leaf on the table. With the faxed information from the Ag Department, he explained everything he knew about the virus. We would divide into two-man teams, wearing protective clothing, and walk every foot of corn along the roads in every field ten rows deep. Any plant that looked infected in the least was to be dug up and placed in the 45-gallon garbage bags. The next day or two would be tough on all of us, and we all knew it. He explained that nobody knew how the virus spread and in as much as the samples had been found along a state highway at Connie's, it apparently was airborne from a truck or vehicle traveling the road. He said he didn't like assumptions, but he had no other explanation as to how it had happened. My stumbling onto the infected plant at a very early stage could make the difference between having a crop or not and Bessie deserved extra oats for wanting to take a walk.

That comment brought the first chuckling of the evening.

All of the families had received letters from grandchildren that day, but their happiness was subdued because of the virus problem.

Three days later, the searching was completed and Connie's field was the only one infected. When Connie and I completed searching her field, we continued farther up and down the road to other cornfields on the neighboring farms and found small areas of contamination on them that the owners weren't aware of. We informed all of them about the virus and how we were dealing with the problem. We asked that they pass the word onto their neighbors.

Phil informed the County Ag Department about the issue and they established a search all along the highway route. Every so often, infected corn was found. Phil theorized that infected corn had been trucked along the highway in an open dump truck and particles had blown off and landed in random cornfields along the way. Phil was determined to find the source. He asked other farmers in the county, especially those who had feeder cattle or milk cows, if they had purchased any corn for their livestock—and the answers were all negative. The search was about to stop, when one cattle farmer said he had purchased a load of corn silage from a young farmer down toward Lincoln. He gave the young farmer's name and address to the County Ag Department and a team of inspectors went to that farm and found silos filled with infected corn. The young farmer had made only one sale of his extra silage. Because of Phil's persistence, the source had been located and the State Health and Ag Departments took over, assisted by a team from the U.S. Department of Agriculture. The farm was put under quarantine and they would determine how the silage was to be removed and to where. It was decided that it be transported in enclosed, sealed containers and taken to a hazardous-waste dumpsite. The young farmer had to sell off his livestock at a loss because he no longer had any feed for his cattle. The young fellow was seeing his dream of being successful go down the drain and there wasn't a thing he could do about it. Fortunately, all of the infected farms had successfully removed the bad corn before it had become a major disaster.

After that week's traumatic potential disaster, the McGregor families gathered for their normal Sunday afternoon of fun. I suggested that since there was now communication with their children, maybe they invite their children and families home for the Fourth of July holiday, and their grandkids could stay and spend the summer. Everyone thought that was a great idea. That evening, phone calls would be made to their kids.

George's, Phil's, and Connie's children all accepted the invitation and plans were made for their arrival in about two weeks. The expected joy of having all of the families together for the holiday became contagious, and even I was excited. I especially wanted to meet Angie and Ann.

Soon the Fourth of July arrived. During the holiday and weeks later, the families' spirits and joy rose to an all-time high. Every day was like a celebration. The older grandkids slept in tents in the backyards. There were campfires, hot dog roasts, toasted marshmallows, and songs sung by everybody topped off with all of the grandchildren topping off each night with a mouth-organ jam session.

The parents had to return home, but kids remained and the grandmothers couldn't spend enough time with the grandchildren. The kids loved the attention and loving bonds were created that would last forever.

Ann, Angie and I got together one afternoon while the kids were taking their nap and we had some hearty laughs over the turmoil they had gone through.

Chapter 39

THE TWO GRAIN CROPS, WINTER WHEAT AND OATS, were within days of harvesting when I started to get that funny feeling again. I didn't know what it was about. My eyes kept looking to the sky. Maybe something to do with the weather? I was feeling nervous.

At the campfire that night, I told Phil I had a funny feeling and it was getting stronger every day. Could we sneak off to the computer for a short time so he could pull up the national weather app for a look-see?

We excused ourselves and went inside. Phil had the computer up and running and the national weather map was on screen. Nebraska looked fine, fair skies and no rain. Phil zoomed out and everything looked fine all the way to the ocean. I asked Phil to check the ocean to the California coast. When that area popped on the screen, my heartbeat increased enough that I noticed it. I pointed to an air pressure depression over the Pacific Ocean and told him that would be a bad problem for us in a few days. It had something to do with the wheat and oats. They had to be harvested at once or they would be lost.

He turned, looked at me, and asked if I was sure. I

nodded and said that was what my gut feeling was telling me. He called the farmers who had helped us with the hay harvest to ask if their combines were ready to roll. Phil said he didn't have time to work out the wages for them, but it would be a fair deal. Phil said starting time would be ten o'clock and to bring their grain wagons. Everything was set for six combines to harvest the wheat first and then the oats, before moving to Connie's farm.

As the grandkids enjoyed themselves by the campfire, Phil explained the situation to the adults. The girls knew that grain harvesting was coming up soon, but a twelve-hour notice took them by surprise. Theresa said, "Let's get all the grandkids together tomorrow morning. George can take the tractor and grain wagons to Phil's tonight, and somebody can bring him back home because I need to stay with the grandkids and get them to bed." I said I would do the same with Connie's tractor and wagons and we should be ready to start combining at ten o'clock or sooner. The party was ended and the fire doused with water. Everyone headed home.

The next morning, six combines, twelve grain wagons, and six tractors headed for the wheat field. Harvesting began. When Phil's wheat and oats were harvested, the equipment was refueled and taken to Connie's farm. Tomorrow her wheat and oats would be harvested, and the following day it would be George's.

An on-field meeting was called and it was agreed that when George's was completed, we would go to the neighbors and do their fields also. George and Phil told the neighbors of the plan and they graciously accepted the offer. They said their harvest was nothing like the McGregors' and wouldn't take as long. As it turned out, twelve fields had been harvested in five days and the Weather Channel showed a massive weather front heading toward Nebraska. It was expected to strike the David City area in the evening, which it did. Massive black clouds extending to 10,000 feet could be seen off to the west and everybody headed home with their equipment at high speed.

As the storm got nearer, thunderclaps could be heard and all of the TV stations were showing severe weather warnings, telling people to take cover. Flash flood warnings were posted on the screen. I called George and Phil and told them to get everything off their basement floors because they would likely have flooded basements by the time the storm ended.

As it turned out, almost every home in the area, especially old farmhouses with original stone foundations, were flooded. High winds, lightning strikes on power transformers, and blown down trees caused total power outages in the David City area. Old oil lamps, long in storage, were brought out and put to use; as well as antique slop jars and buckets filled with water to flush the toilets and for drinking. Suddenly, the countryside was like it is was in the 1880s. Wood-burning stoves and fireplaces were used for cooking and everyone huddled into one large room in the house. The heaviest part of the storm lasted for almost six hours before it slowly moved to the east. Rainfall records were shattered by this massive storm.

People who had battery-operated radios listened to condition reports for the county. The Nebraska State Police had their helicopters reporting on conditions of the roads and highways and telling people to stay off the roads as bridges were washed out and flash flooding was everywhere. No emergency vehicles could travel in the county and if any rescues had to made it would have to be by helicopter. All communication was gone except for cell phones and people were told not to use them except for an emergency in order to save their batteries. No emergency planning had prepared people for operating under these conditions and the Governor of Nebraska flew up from Lincoln to see the devastation. He declared the area a disaster zone. It would be days before power would be restored and power company crews were brought in to try and restore power as quickly as possible.

The McGregors had generators and Phil and I got them hooked up and running. Using his big tractor, Phil got to Connie's house by pulling massive trees out of the roadway with logging chains. I got into his cab and we set out for George's home where we connected a generator to his house. The grandchildren had been terribly frightened and the girls were still trying to calm them down that next morning. Once the generators were hooked up and running, and a hot breakfast had been served by the girls, the grandchildren finally started to relax. Phil and I left George's to open the road to the three farmers that had helped us and George followed with his truck, towing a generator and electrical wire that was used to irrigate the fields.

They were happy to see us with the portable generator in tow! When one household was hooked up and running, George drove back to his farm and hooked onto another wagon and generator. The three of us continued all day. All fifteen generators the McGregors owned were loaned out. Our biggest problem was avoiding the downed power and telephone lines that were lying on the roadways.

While we were gone, Connie and Julie took the grandchildren to the milking parlor and taught the kids how to milk a cow. They had a lot of stories to tell of that experience. Theresa Marie, Connie, and Julie called their kids to let the grandchildren talk with their parents. The parents could hardly believe their city kids could milk cows. Every child had to tell their cousins about the storm and how many cows they had milked—and the kids had a way of increasing the number of cows they had milked that day. For years, those stories would be repeated; and, in time, would be repeated to their children. Their fears had vanished and happiness prevailed once again.

The next day, the sun came out strong and hot. The humidity shot way up and then the air was very muggy, but the kids ran and jumped with bare feet in the mud puddles as entertainment. The scariness of the storm was forgotten.

The storm had bent the cornstalks sideways, but they were more vertical than horizontal, which was good because the corn ears could still develop; so the crop was not lost. It might be a problem doing the picking as slower speeds might be necessary. The soy bean and hay seemed okay. The biggest problem was the standing water in the fields. If it stayed hot, then it was likely the standing water would evaporate faster than it could soak into the soil. One certainty, at least for a while, was we wouldn't be tied down irrigating the fields.

The McGregor fields survived the storm flooding quite well because the crops helped stop severe eroding of the topsoil. The harvested wheat and oat fields had washouts and gullies from water rushing to low spots in the fields. Loading buckets would be mounted to the front of the tractors and the field could be rebuilt.

One problem was the basements of all three farmhouses had been badly flooded. First, the bulk water was removed and then shop wet-vacs were used to remove almost all of the remaining water, leaving damp floors to be mopped. Bleach water was sprayed from a tank sprayer onto the fieldstone walls and on the cement floor to kill any mildew and mold that might begin to form. The basement windows were opened and the outside entrance door was opened. In the basements, box fans were turned on high to ventilate the area. After a week of ventilating, the fans could be shut down. Dehumidifiers had to be purchased to remove remaining humidity to at least to 55%, further drying out the contained air. The third day after the storm, a good stiff, dry wind from the west blew over the area and the humidity dropped which helped evaporate the standing water from the fields. Two or three days of the wind blowing and the hay might be ready to cut and bail and the soybeans wouldn't suffer from mold and mildew. The soil was too wet to cultivate the corn; so that job was delayed. Instead we worked on the combines to get them ready to use.

The third week in July, the grandkids' parents would begin to arrive to take their kids back home as many of them had to return to school in August. The kids had investigated every barn and found something of interest in each one. They enjoyed climbing the ladders that rose to the peak of the old-style barns and jumping onto the bales of hay stacked below. Climbing a vertical ladder was a new experience for them.

The poor milk cows that were used to quiet serenity, found themselves subjected to all kinds of treatments, like a kid moving its tail up and down like it was like a handle on a hand pump. Grandpa always knew when the kids had been messing with the cows because that evening the milk production dropped from normal. The hogs never had to suffer because they would chase the kids from their pasture and the kids would run for their lives and jump the fence just in time.

In the granary the kids liked to slide their hand through the freshly harvested wheat and oats while noticing the different feel of the grains. The girls would go with Grandma to feed the chickens and tell them about how chickens lived, laid eggs, pecked the soil for bugs or seedlings, and drink water.

One by one, as the parents arrived, they were guided around the farm by their kids. Every kid had a deep tan and hair that almost reached his or her shoulders. I think every child asked their grandparents if they could return next summer—and all of the grandparents said absolutely. It might take Grandma and Grandpa fifty weeks to recover, but the kids would be welcomed with open arms.

~ ~ ~

After the children and parents left, the six of us crashed into comfortable chairs and told stories about what we had just gone through. All five grandparents had enjoyed every minute and a loving bond now existed between them and their grandchildren.

About this time, I started feeling uneasy with myself. At first, I didn't understand why. Each day, the uneasiness was a little greater and I began to withdraw into myself. Something was going on mentally with me; so one morning I thought I would check out Susie for tire pressure and oil level in the engine. It had been a long time since she was last serviced—and it dawned on me that my inner self was wanting to return home to Northport.

The more I thought about it, the stronger the urge. The problem was, I didn't want to leave Connie. I wanted her with me. Our relationship had become very close and I couldn't just drive away without hurting her feelings—that was the last thing I wanted to do. She had a big farm to manage and had counted on me every day, it seemed. I couldn't lie to her and give her some lame excuse that I had things to do at home. She would know better. My makeup was never to tell a lie; to tell the truth no matter what, and take whatever I had coming.

The big question was how to break the news. As I tried to figure out how, I became more withdrawn. I was coming up empty-handed. I planned to head for home on August third. Each day became more difficult. Soon, August third would arrive. How would I tell Connie what the problem was?

Chapter 40

IT WAS SATURDAY, JULY 30. IN FOUR DAYS I WOULD BE leaving and I had not told Connie of my plans. I wasn't being fair to her. Somehow I had to find a way. I withdrew into myself even more.

It had been a beautiful day. After chores and dinner, Connie and I sat in the swing looking out toward the western horizon, over the cornstalks, enjoying the view. We each had a mug of coffee and hardly said a word to each other as the sun sank lower. She took my hand in hers, looked straight at me, and said, "What's troubling you? You've been so withdrawn all week. Is it something I have done?"

Connie had given me an opening to explain, if I could, what my plans were. I answered, "Heavens, no! The problem is with me. And I don't know how to tell you what's the matter."

"You've always told me to start at the beginning," she said, "and the words will come."

"The last thing I want to do is hurt your feelings," I said. "What I say might have a sting to it; so let me tell you how I feel, what I feel I must do, and please don't interrupt me until I have finished. Then, do what is best for you—not me. Okay?"

Connie nodded yes.

"I believe we have an unspoken love for each other that has grown ever since I arrived at your door." Just then the phone inside the house rang. Connie did not move to answer it. "You have always been gracious and kind to me in every way, and I appreciate it more than I can explain. I've always tried to return that kindness to you every day, and a friendship has grown between us over the last six months. I think we depend on each other in every way. We are sad together, laugh together, and do so many things together; I think we support each other in whatever we are doing.

"We sometimes hold hands, hug, and even give quick kisses to each other. Right now, we have feelings for each other that are ultimate in any kind of relationship—and again, I think we have come to love each other. The problem is, I'm like a migrating bird that feels it must fly south when winter is coming and fly north when spring arrives. They're not drifters, just birds that do what inwardly they feel they must do.

"I have been feeling an urge to return home ever since the children left, and I haven't found a way to tell you. I will not just drive away and leave you. My feelings inside are telling me I must return to Northport. I feel I now have two homes, one in Northport and one here, with you."

At that point the sun was almost set.

"I need your help because my eyesight is failing and I have no idea how long I will have it. Soon I will be considered blind and I will have difficulty caring for myself. All of my life I've always tried to help others solve problems, but this one problem I can't solve. The biggest problem is I don't want to burden you because it will be 24/7 support and it will drag you down mentally and physically. At least, that is what I believe.

"I guess I'm asking for help and also declining your help at the same time. If we part company, we will always feel the same as we do now, I hope. If you want to join me in Northport, I will have eyesight long enough to explore the countryside and waters of Lake Michigan together. Then, we could return to your home for the spring and summer. It's a terribly tough decision for you to make, and I want you to take your time. I don't need to have an answer right now."

The sun disappeared in the horizon as I finished the last sentence. Connie got up from the swing; I thought she was walking away from me. Instead, she uncrossed my legs, sat on my lap, put her arms around me, and our heads were together. This had been terrible and I was glad my feelings had been expressed. Tears flowed down my checks and onto my shirt. I just sat frozen, not wanting to move. Tears started flowing from her eyes also and we each gripped each other not saying a word. We were both too emotional to speak. We just clutched each other in silence.

Dusk arrived, then total darkness. The only light was from the kitchen door behind us. I don't know how long we sat there crying like babies. No words needed to be said because I knew she would ride away from the farm and all of its problems. She wanted to be with me. I told her I loved her and she replied the same.

After more time elapsed, I said she had better return the phone call before it got any later and I would go to Bessie with her evening sugar treats. We both went inside the house. I got some treats and told Connie when she got done talking I would be at the barnyard gate. I turned on the yard light and went to the barnyard, she started talking on the phone. With the yard light on, Bessie saw me walking toward her and she got up and met me at the gate for her treats. I gave her two sugar cubes and she started nuzzling my hand for more. I rubbed her around the ears and scratched her muzzle and she stood there and soaked it all in.

About ten minutes later, Connie came up to me, turned me so we were facing each other, and we kissed for the longest time. There was no question we were in love. Eventually we stopped kissing and she said it was Theresa Marie. She told Theresa Marie she was leaving for Michigan Wednesday morning and Phil and George would have to manage the farm and crops. George was to take Bessie to their farm and the chickens were to be split between Julie and her. The packing of clothes would start on Monday, and Sunday would be spent going to church, a jam session, and dessert afterward just like always.

"What about your kids? How will they feel?" I asked.

"There's no problem," Connie said. "Before they left to go home they said they really liked you and that you were good for me. They welcomed you into the family. They said they owed you more than a lot for getting the family back together."

That night we made an unspoken commitment to each other and our hearts were filled with unmeasurable joy and happiness.

Chapter 41

SUNDAY WAS A TYPICAL SUNDAY UNTIL AFTER THE afternoon jam session when George and Phil returned their instruments to their vehicles. I asked what type of dinnerware was wanted for the dessert and Theresa Marie replied, "Dinner plates, forks, and spoons." It seemed unusual for a dinner plate but I obliged and set the table.

George returned from the truck carrying a big sheet cake and Phil carried a large pie plate. Both were set in the middle of the dining room table. Connie came in with a big tub of strawberry ice cream and the girls uncovered the cake and pie. On the cake was lettered "Congratulations Connie and Trev" with homemade strawberry frosting with red frosting roses. Theresa Marie said the cake was made from fresh-picked strawberries. Julie had baked an eleven-inch pie from fresh-picked strawberries and rhubarb from her garden. The ice cream was butter pecan that they had purchased.

Julie said not to cut the cake and pie yet because she wanted to take some pictures of the occasion, with Connie and me in the pictures. This was a going-away and congratulation feast for the two of us. She had no idea what Theresa Marie and Julie had literally cooked up. We all ate heartily and made a big dent in both the cake and the pie. Of course, George, Phil, and I had to have seconds. We were all stuffed and sitting in our chairs when they sang "For There're Jolly Good Fellows" and it left Connie and me speechless. We clapped our hands in appreciation.

Julie said not to worry about the food. On Wednesday, she and Theresa Marie would take care of what should be removed. Both their families had keys to the house. Bessie and the chickens would be moved to their homes. Laughing, I said I would like to be there when George and Phil tried to corral the chickens into a cage. That would be comical to see. The girls broke into laughter as they visualized what was going to happen. George and Phil had a funny face of displeasure as they suddenly realized what they were in for.

After everyone left, I picked up the dishes and together Connie and I cleaned up the kitchen.

The next morning, all of the winter clothing was gathered together, including the winter boots I had arrived in in January. Connie boiled eggs for snacking on while we were on the road, fresh bread was baked, and a jar of Concord grape jelly. Its label said: "Packaged in Paw Paw, Michigan." Connie asked, "Where in the world is Paw Paw?"

I said about fifteen miles west of Kalamazoo.

"Where is Kalamazoo?" she asked.

In jest, I answered, "In Kalamazoo County."

What a look she gave me! I told her Kalamazoo was halfway between Chicago and Detroit in Southern Michigan, and it was where I was born and that we would be going there to visit Kay's grave and to see the monument that also had my name cast into it. We would also drive by the house where I grew up and the home in the country that Kay and I built with our own hands. I said that was house number one. We constructed two more houses together and house number two was the house Connie and I were going to live in.

My adventure had lasted almost seven months. I had met many wonderful people along the way and I had kept a journal of what happened each day, including the months I spent with the McGregors.

Having love enter my life made it a wonderful adventure.

The End